BACK LASH

USA Today Bestselling author Devon Monk returns to her gritty, magic-fueled, urban fantasy adventure. Cursed with Life and Death magic, enemies-to-brothers fight for dominance in a city full of bad guys that have no idea who they're up against. *Fully updated author edition: bursting with Heart, Snark, and Ass-kicking.*

Shame Flynn and Terric Conley hadn't meant to become the living, breathing vessels for Death and Life magic. But they hadn't meant to die, be reborn, break magic, save the world, and kill a few psychopaths along the way, either.

The one thing they *had* meant to do was to seal

magic away once and for all, so it could never be used to kill again.

But when a string of dead bodies—people killed by magic—appear throughout Portland, Oregon, Shame and Terric must scramble to uncover who broke the locks on magic this time, and how.

And they need to do it fast. Before Terric's sister becomes the next target, before the Russian mob locks them in their sights. And before an innocent child and her foolish father accidentally put themselves on the magic battlefield that will only get them killed.

BACK LASH

BROKEN MAGIC
BOOK 3

DEVON MONK

ODD
HOUSE
PRESS

CHAPTER 1

Some people just don't die easy.

I should know. I, Shamus Flynn, had died several times—all of them the hard way.

Being the only person in the world who carried Death magic came with a catch. Death magic needed to be fed, needed to devour life. It got all kinds of stabby when it didn't get what it wanted.

Most of the time I managed it and managed myself so that I didn't go full-on Grim Reaper.

Occasionally I slipped. And that meant some unlucky bastard was in for a very bad day.

I wasn't alone in this magic-user thing though. My not-best friend, work partner, and unwelcome-room-mate, Terric Conley was my opposite: a Life magic user who, I admitted only in my darkest moments, I couldn't function without.

The tie Life and Death magic had welded between us—the Soul Complement—was unbreakable.

Trust me, we'd tried breaking it.

I was a walking, talking Grim Reaper, and he was the vessel of healing and life.

Yin-yang. Beauty and the beast. Cancer and cure.

He and I had once been the head of magic here in Portland, Oregon. Before we'd been fired, hunted, tortured, killed (then had saved the world, and destroyed magic) and were finally, painfully reborn.

Good times.

But out of all that, we had made one thing happen: no one could access magic any more. No one could offer up a little pain and draw a spell glyph and expect magic to jump to.

Magic flowed like water through channels beneath the cities and land. It flowed especially strong beneath Portland.

That magic used to be as simple to tap as turning on a faucet.

Not anymore. Terric and I had put an end to that extraordinarily easy, dangerous access.

Which is why the half-naked dead guy slumped in the pile of garbage in the alley in front of me was such a surprise.

This corpse—a fat man in designer slacks and new shoes who looked like he had clenched it just this side of sixty—had the glyphs for Pain and Surrender and Binding burned across his forehead, chest, and throat.

Burned into his flesh with magic, not fire.

Brutal and effective magic work.

A hell of a gruesome way to go.

Well, then. Someone had been a bad boy, and it wasn't me for a change. What was the world coming to?

Here's the thing: no one can use magic except Terric and me.

What? A couple blokes die to save the world and they can't slip a little loophole into the new rules?

Plus, being the only people who could stir the magic pot wasn't for kicks. Magic still demanded a price for using it, and that price was still pain.

Constant pain.

"Don't know what you did to piss off Mr. Nice Guy," I said to the corpse. I dug in my hoodie pocket for a cig and a light. "But it's going to be all sorts of delightful to watch him try to talk his way out of his 'no more killing, Shame' rule."

I glanced at both ends of the alley. Normal non-magical people walked the street doing normal non-magical things in the normal, dear-God-so-damn *normal* non-magical spring day. No one paid attention to me because, frankly, I looked like I belonged in the alley: dark hair in need of a cut, black hoodie, fingerless gloves, jeans, boots.

Lean, angry, broken. It all described me.

But that wasn't all I was.

I lit my cigarette, sucked the destruction of paper and tobacco into lungs, then deeper, feeding it to the gnawing, bottomless hunger of Death magic inside me. One burning cig wasn't much to feed the need for death that pounded like a second pulse behind my throat, my eyes, my mouth.

But it wasn't nothing.

These days I took every bit of death I could get.

I exhaled smoke, then *tsked*.

"Leaving those marks behind is just...sloppy." I crouched next to the corpse to get a better look. Noticed a tattoo obscured by the Binding glyph over his heart. Maybe the head of a dragon, maybe a fish? Something that looked like it came out of a tourist stall in Chinatown.

"It's not like people don't remember that they used to use magic. It's only been off limits for a year. Am I right, buddy?"

The corpse, being dead, didn't say anything, and there was no ghost left behind either—something I was happy about.

"Why would you only half-strip a guy, Terric?" I muttered around the cigarette in my mouth. I took a moment, sucked the flame deep, burned a column of ash. Held my breath. Tossed the butt over my shoulder into the wet of moss and slime.

"You like your men all the way naked," I continued on the exhale. "And a hell of a lot younger than this guy. And leaner." I took a good look at his face. "And better looking. So, I'm going to guess this wasn't a lover's spat."

I slid a finger in the dead guy's front pockets. No I.D.

Pivoted on my boots, scanning the alley for the man's shirt and coat. Nothing.

"The more I look at this..." I tipped my head up, checked roof lines for movement, cameras, guns. No, no, and no.

"...the more I think you, Deadguy, are a setup to frame someone for murder."

I stood, weighed my options.

"What I want to know is who the hell has access to that much magic and can use life-ending spells without killing themselves in the process. Other than Terric. What poor chump was supposed to get nailed for your murder?"

I tugged the phone out of my pocket. Snapped a picture of the guy.

Then I leaned down over the top of him. I placed the heel of my palm against the Pain glyph on his forehead. That glyph was not a joke, not a fake. That was a spell burned into his flesh. A very deadly spell.

I called on the knot of magic inside me and let it pour out through my hand to eat away at that spell. Left a bloody mess and the smell of rotten oranges and old ass behind. Did the same to his throat and chest.

Stood back to check my handiwork. Looked like he'd put acid in his body spray.

At least it didn't look like death by magic.

Good enough.

What I should do was call Terric, find out what he had to say about all this. What I *could* do was hit the pub and get my liquid lunch on.

Since there was plenty of day left, and I was pretty sure it was gonna take a couple beers to get the taste of magic-fried corpse out of my mouth, I headed to the pub.

CHAPTER 2

"All of them," Terric said, sliding the sheet of paper across the kitchen table toward me. "Every last one." He snapped a pen down on the paper and leaned back in his chair, watching me through narrow, angry eyes.

Terric was, in many ways, my opposite. Clean-shaven and fashionably dressed. White hair recently chopped for a short, messy look, blue eyes, and straight-up Hollywood handsome. Also, he was responsible, fair-minded, and even-tempered.

"Formal interrogation before breakfast?" I waved my coffee cup his way. "You and Dash fighting again?"

The soft chime of dry cereal pouring into a glass bowl behind me paused. Dashiell Spade—Terric's boyfriend—sighed, then filled a second bowl. "We're not fighting. Trying to change the subject won't hide the fact that you're killing people, Shame."

Dash came around the table and placed a bowl of cereal in front of me and one in front of Terric. He was dark-haired, light-skinned, and wore black-framed glasses that accented his moss green eyes. I noted he didn't touch Terric's shoulder like usual, noted Terric's steady gaze on mine did not flick up to acknowledge Dash.

I'd been throwing shit about them fighting. But it looked like I'd hit the bull's-eye.

"You both know I've killed," I said. "Mr. Death magic, right here."

Dash pulled the milk out of the refrigerator and placed that on the table too. I was watching Terric not watch Dash. Raised my eyebrow in question.

He blinked, shook his head slightly. That, along with the Soul Complement bond between us, let me know he didn't want to talk about whatever was wrong with the two of them.

It would have been easy to bring it up. To throw their possibly first argument and relationship snarl out on the breakfast table. It would have taken the heat off them accusing me of killing someone I had not killed.

But thing is, I liked Dash. He was smart, knew when to keep his mouth shut, and had been invaluable when Ter and I had been dealing with the fallout from the Authority—a secret society of magic users—going public. All the good, bad, and terrible things that secret society had done had become public knowledge, and the public had not liked it one bit.

I owed Dash a little something for standing beside Terric and me when all hell was coming loose and anyone who remained near us was just putting themselves in the blast zone.

So for Dash—not Terric—I let go of the easy way out.

What can I say? I'm maturing as a person.

"All of the people you've killed for the last year," Terric said, with a little less anger.

Dash still hadn't sat down to breakfast. He stood at the toaster as if fascinated by the browning of bread between coils.

I flicked a look at the blank paper and the pen. There was no way in hell I was going to tell him how many people I'd killed in the last year.

Yes, I killed people. Horrible, right? Monstrous? I don't disagree.

But the Death magic burning in me demanded to be fed. If I didn't choose what death to shovel into that fire, Death magic took what it wanted. Devoured and destroyed with random, brutal efficiency.

Innocent people died if I didn't give death its due. So, I made sure to only take out the people who had committed magical crimes so terrible they'd gotten their memories wiped by the Authority.

Killing by magic was a bit more difficult now. For one thing, the criminals had all regained their wiped memories when the Authority went public. Having found out they had been removed from their lives, sometimes given new personalities, new jobs, new memories, didn't make a single one of them happy. But the criminals had already been tried, judged, and sentenced. Taking their memories was a mercy killing back when the Authority was in full swing.

I was just taking care of old business.

"Nope," I said. "Not going to happen."

Terric waited, measuring me. That Soul Complement bond worked both ways. If he was paying attention, he knew just how much nope I was about to throw at this.

He took a breath, sat back and lifted the fingers of one hand. "Just the last three months. It's important."

I slurped coffee, watched him jerk when the toaster popped. Watched him not look over while Dash scraped butter across toast and spread marmalade.

This was amusing, but also ridiculous.

"You going to eat on your feet today?" I asked Dash.

He carried a plate over to the table and sat in the only other chair, between us.

"It's none of your business what's bothering us,

Shame," he said, getting right to the point of what *I* was not talking about, and *they* were not ignoring.

He poured milk into Terric's bowl while giving Terric a pointed look. "We'll figure it out."

Dash wasn't a part of our Soul Complement bond, but he was a smart man. He knew Terric and I had been not talking about them.

"What we don't have figured out," he continued, "is why you're knocking off people and leaving them out in the open with magic burned into them. How is that in any way smart?"

"It isn't," Terric said. "It's sloppy and stupid. You might be one of those things, but you are never both. What in the hell is wrong with you?"

"*I'm* not the one leaving dead bodies in alleyways."

Terric exhaled a short breath and shook his head. "Don't play this game."

"Game? No," I said. "Uh-uh. You are not going to do the dirty and blame it on me. *I* didn't leave anyone dead in an alley, obviously killed by magic."

"Bullshit."

"The man doth protest too loudly," I said.

"I'm not stupid enough to leave a body out in the open."

"And I am?"

"I'm not the one who has a goddamn hit list in my pocket."

I took a drink of coffee, mostly to bother Terric and to give myself a moment to consider what he'd said. The coffee went ice cold in my hands, Death magic inside me sucking out the heat of it. He was right to suspect me. I did have a hit list.

So, Terric didn't do it. Or wanted me to think he didn't. Why?

"Half-naked man isn't exactly my style," I observed calmly, watching his reaction.

"Who said anything about half-naked?"

"The man in the alley I found yesterday was stripped to his slacks. Half-naked."

Terric lifted his head, his eyes searching my face. He knew I wasn't lying. He should sense that through our connection too.

"You found?" he said. "Yesterday?"

I nodded. I was watching Terric, but also keeping tabs on Dash out of the corner of my eye.

Terric and I were the only people in Portland who could use magic. As far as we knew, we were the only people in the world who could use magic at all. We'd been pretty clear about that loophole we'd slipped into the new rules of magic when we'd locked magic away.

Only he and I got to play with the cool toys.

Dash was the one person who knew we could access magic. He looked slightly shocked and more than a little sick.

"In an alley off of Burnside," I went on. "I didn't kill the guy. I did clean up the magic marks. Burned them off so when the cops found him, they'd find a bloody, but not a magic mess. Are you sure you want to tell me you didn't do it, Ter?"

"I don't kill people," he said. Through our bond, I heard what he didn't say: *like that*.

"Well, neither do I," I said. "Like that. Which means we have a problem, boys."

"No one can access magic," Dash said.

"Someone did," I said.

"Maybe it just looks like a magic kill?" he suggested. He glanced over at Terric, who was staring at me, and then he looked back at me, staring at Terric.

"It was a magic kill," Terric said.

"I wasn't a part of it," I repeated. "Did you touch the corpse, Ter? Did you get a read for what kind of magic was used? Did you sense me in it at all?"

"I touched him."

"And?"

"Healed him."

I drank coffee while I let that set in. "You healed a dead guy." It wasn't a question, but some things just needed to be said out loud.

"Life magic," he noted.

I nodded. I hadn't ever thought through his need to pour life into the world as far as healing the dead.

Raising the dead? Maybe. Mending dead flesh? Creepy.

"Cause of death?" I asked.

"Cops will think it's a heart attack. The guy on Burnside?"

"Mugging with an acid burn chaser."

"Did you recognize the signature?"

I dug in my pocket for my phone. "I didn't look at it that closely since I thought it had to be you. Took a picture, though."

"Shit," Terric said. "I should have thought of that."

"I did." Dash pulled his phone out of his pocket.

"You took a picture of me healing the corpse?" Terric looked over at him for the first time today. Dash was flipping through photos, so didn't notice.

"Just the glyphs. Something seemed...off about them. Too neat. Too...practiced for Shame."

"Hey, I'm practiced."

"No, you're experienced. There was something so...Sunday school about these glyphs."

"Surrender and Pain do fit the Sunday school motif."

The corner of Dash's mouth twitched up. "No, I mean they looked like they were cast by someone who had never practiced magic before."

Terric made a *hmm* sound and leaned forward. Dash turned the screen so he could study the picture.

"He's right," Terric said. "I don't know why I didn't notice it before."

"You were too busy outlining how you were going to kick Shame's ass."

"Aw. Nice to know you care, Ter," I said. "Let's see."

Dash turned the phone my way. This dead guy was thinner, younger, lighter hair. Slightly familiar.

"Do we know him?" I asked.

Terric shook his head. "I don't. You?"

I shrugged. Slid my phone across the table for him. "When did you find him?"

"Day before last," Dash said. "Out off of Lombard."

"And you waited this long to accuse me?" I finished my coffee. "Going soft, boys?"

"Giving you a chance to come clean." Terric frowned down at my phone. "Have you ever seen this man before?"

"No."

"Was there any ID on him?"

"Nope."

"Same with ours." Terric leaned back and steepled his fingers. It was the pose our mentor, Victor, had often assumed when he was trying to think through a tough question. I hadn't realized Terric had picked it up.

"Was he inked?" I asked.

"I didn't notice," Terric said.

Dash shook his head. "Was yours?"

"Yes. Under the glyph for Binding on his chest. A reptile or fish of some kind."

Dash thumbed through the pictures on his phone again, zooming in on them. "Nothing I can see."

"So that's a dead end," I said. "Where do we go from here?"

"Davy and Sunny?" Dash offered into the silence.

Davy and Sunny were friends of ours who had stood beside us even though that meant Davy had been kidnapped and very nearly beaten to death when we'd taken on the people who wanted to use magic—and people who could use magic—for very bad things.

The two were in love, and used to be Hounds—people who could track illegal magic use back to the user. But since magic had been locked up for a year now, the Hounding business had pretty much dried up. Last I'd heard, they'd decided to get married and get out of the magical private detecting business altogether.

"Rather not drag them into it," I said. "They've paid enough prices."

"Agreed," Terric said. "And I'm not certain they'd have anything to offer us in the way of tracking this down."

"They'd have records," Dash suggested.

"We have records," I said. "You didn't just burn all the info we had on every magic user in the Pacific Northwest when we got fired, did you, Dash? Maybe you kept a file? A flash drive or two?"

Dash inhaled and narrowed his eyes while he considered that. I gave him an innocent look. I expected Dash had indeed done the right thing and deleted all the files we used to have access to back when we were running the no-longer-secret Authority.

But the thing is, with great knowledge comes great cover-ups. And the Authority was excellent at cover-ups.

Like, say, when someone found out a little too much about the secret side of magic. The Authority's response was to wipe their memories, take away their ability to use magic, and give them a new life.

Witness protection program with a twist—you didn't know you were in a witness protection program because you couldn't remember who you used to be.

Nasty business, that.

Nastier now that everyone—and I mean every lovely, horrible, brutal, vengeful person—had gotten their memories back.

"I'm going to bet you kept a little something just in case of emergencies, eh, mate?" I said. "For protection?"

"I don't need protection," Dash said.

"No. But you knew Terric might, right?"

Dash shot me an angry look and I was reminded that the man knew how to fight. Might even want to show me some pointers over the kitchen table.

What had I said to piss him off?

"You know I couldn't save any of the records," Dash snarled. "Not even if I wanted to. Not even for Terric."

"Wow," I said.

The silence stretched a moment. Dash was not the short-tempered sort. That was the biggest outburst I'd ever heard from him.

I couldn't help but smile. Something was under his skin and I was pretty sure it wasn't me.

"Dash," Terric asked, "what did you keep?"

"I just told you. Nothing."

I nodded, pulled my phone back into my palm, then pocket. "So, you're lying. Obvious. Do I need to point that out, or are we just going to let it go until old records we didn't know still existed suddenly appear on our doorstep?"

"If it's not records," Terric said, throwing me a warning scowl, "what are you worried about?"

"Nothing. It's...nothing." Now it was Dash's turn to glare at me. "Why do you have to make everything harder than it is?"

"Daddy issues?" I offered. "Poor boundaries as a child? Death magic eating my soul?"

"Not. Funny." Dash stood. "As a matter of fact, I don't think you've ever been funny, Shame. I need some air."

With that, he walked out of the kitchen, grabbed his coat off the hook by the door and left, slamming the door behind him.

I stared after him a minute. I could count on zero fingers exactly how many times I'd seen Dash storm out like that.

"Wow," I said again. "Is it the sex? You two fighting over who gets to be the little spoon?"

"He got a job offer." Terric rubbed his eyes.

"For sex? Shouldn't you get a cut of that?"

He let his hand drop and just stared at the table, ignoring me.

Ah. So this was serious.

"Okay," I said. "What's the problem with the job?"

"It's in Canada."

"Did you tell him not to take it?" I stood. Magic in me was sharp and hungry and I needed to move a bit to take my focus off it.

Death magic wasn't hungry for food. I needed to kill something or someone. Soon.

"No," Terric said, as I poured coffee that instantly went cold. "I told him he should take it. He should go."

I set the pot back on the warmer and turned, leaning against the counter behind me.

Sunlight swung in through the window, washing Terric's face in a watercolor of light. Shadows of wind-stirred leaves slid down his eyes, his hands.

He was holding himself very, very still. I couldn't feel anything through our connection except silence.

But I knew behind his silence was pain.

"Is he leaving?" I asked quietly.

"He's angry."

"I can see that. Because you told him to take the job?"

He shrugged one shoulder. "Because I told him to go."

"Is that what you want?"

The silence between us churned. So much pain behind it. And heartache. Jesus. Terric loved that man.

"You know," I said, "I was pretty sure we'd agreed I was the stupid one in this," I waved a hand between us, "bond we have here, not you. You love him, Terric. Go to Canada and be with him."

A sour smile twisted his mouth. "I can't."

He looked up, blue eyes icy with that truth. "This," he mimicked, waving his hand between us, "bond we have here won't let me."

"Bullshit. We're tied together by magic. Doesn't

mean we have to breathe each other's air. It's never meant that."

"Except that it has."

"We don't know that it still works that way."

"We don't know that it doesn't."

"That's because one of us won't move out of my house. Seriously, Terric. Time to spread your wings and get out of my goddamn nest. We'll never know if we can be apart if you don't leave."

He stood, walked over to me until he was standing less than six inches away. "Maybe I don't want to find out what happens when we don't have each other around."

He wrapped his left hand around my coffee cup, which had already gone from cold to ice cold. The cup warmed, grew hot.

Terric didn't let go, didn't stop pouring Life magic in the coffee and cup.

Damn him.

"How long has it been since you killed, Shame?" he asked evenly. "How long since you sated that hollow pit inside you?"

"What year is it? Divide by a decade, carry the forever..."

The cup was too hot to hold. Burning my palm. Terric knew it and just kept pouring heat into it—but it was more than heat.

It was life.

The plants along the window sill shivered and stretched fronds and leaves toward him.

Blisters on my palm broke and instantly healed.

My heart was beating too fast.

So was his.

Magic wasn't a blessing with drawbacks, it was a curse with upsides.

And the upside to being connected to the only other guy who could use magic?

This.

I chewed on my bottom lip, fighting the hunger, which was a stupid old habit.

"Don't be stupid," Terric said. Life magic filled the kitchen, so thick, I could taste the wash of green and sweetness of it.

"I'm not stupid."

Terric smiled, and, yeah, I watched his eyes. It still worried me that I might see there the alien coldness, the full possession of Life magic that made Terric into something glossy and perfect and not-human.

It had happened before.

But that wasn't there. That hadn't been there for a year. I still hadn't gotten used to the idea that using Life magic wouldn't hurt him.

He twitched one eyebrow up, a spark of either

humor or determination burning there. "Prove you've got brains, Death boy."

He stuck his other hand on my chest and pushed hard enough I exhaled.

I hated a dare. He knew that.

I also couldn't resist one. He knew that, too.

Bastard.

"Screw you," I said.

"Shut up and get on with it. I have a client today."

I almost said no. This had been our fallback, our solution to the need of magic that pushed us. A year ago, if either of us let go and used Life or Death magic too much—like this—it pretty quickly turned us into something very different from human.

I became a vessel for death and destruction—an endless, hungry, killing maw. He became a burning, calculating, cold vessel for life, which turned out to be just as destructive as death. So instead, we portioned and cheated. I had my hit list I was making my way through, and Terric did an awful lot of "volunteering" down at the cancer ward and hospitals.

We cheated to get by. But right here, in this damn kitchen, was the kind of honesty I rarely accepted in my life. Right here, was us admitting that we really couldn't be apart from each other, even if we wanted to.

That being together was actually a good thing.

It scared the hell out of me. People who were around me for too long ended up dead, and even though I liked to give him crap, I didn't hate Terric. Didn't want to see him dead.

Far from it.

"Jesus, Terric," I said. "This..."

"We'll worry about it later. I want your head clear. Someone out there is using magic to kill people. *Magic*, Shame. That shouldn't be possible. We made sure...we gave up a hell of a lot—the world gave up a hell of a lot—to make sure that wasn't possible. We are not going to let some crazy person break into magic and use it for murder."

I didn't bring up the fact that I was using magic to kill people too—a horror I justified knowing that the people I killed were criminals who had committed unspeakable magical crimes and would do so again.

If they could access magic.

Which they shouldn't be able to do. The price of using magic is directly proportional to what you want it to do. Want it to kill someone? Well, then someone— usually the magic user—pays the price by dying for that death.

It was the one thing that had kept the magic killing business down to a minimum. But there had been ways around the rules back in the day.

There were always ways around the rules.

Apparently, some guy out there had just discovered a work-around and had used magic to kill.

"Fuck." I lifted my coffee cup away from Terric's hand and took a drink.

Life, pure and strong, filled my mouth and hit me like a truck.

I managed not to moan as I swallowed it down with my coffee. Terric did me the kindness of ignoring my reaction.

He just stood there, his hand on my chest, and pulled out his phone. He stared at the screen while Death magic rose up in me and devoured the Life he offered. Every gulp of coffee was a little headier than the last. I burned my mouth in my haste to get it all down, and didn't care that the burns instantly healed.

When the coffee was gone, I stood there with my eyes closed, pulling in every last ounce of Life I could get.

Terric grunted. "Shit. Okay. That should be enough." He drew his hand away.

But Death magic wanted more.

My eyes snapped open, and I grabbed his wrist.

He pivoted, left fist cocked. He had a good swing at my face if he wanted it.

I don't know what he saw in my expression. I knew what I saw in his: caution and concern. But not fear. We'd pretty much been down to the end of Fear Road and back. We knew we could trust each other. Even at our worst.

This was nowhere near my worst.

I slowly released his wrist.

"Really?" I said. "Violence?"

"It's not like I couldn't have patched you up." He relaxed his fist. "Next time, just ask me for this before you go feral."

"I have never asked you for this."

"And how has that made either of us better? We've been through worse when magic was out in the open. Seems like we can just give each other what we need and not get worked up about it now."

I put my empty cup back on the counter. "I get what I need without you just fine, thanks."

"By killing those people on Victor's hit list?"

He had never asked to see the list, something I was grateful for. I was cautious enough to make the deaths look natural, to space them out so it didn't look suspicious. So far, I didn't think anyone had figured out I was knocking off the worst of the worst of the magic criminals. So far, it was all in control.

"And?" I asked.

"And what are you going to do when that list runs out, Shame?"

Yes, I'd thought about that. As a matter of fact, that question was a re-occurring nightmare that woke me in the middle of the night. That question had forced me to slow down on the killing thing—way, way down—and to hold off between big kills with much, much smaller deaths. Plants, bugs, rodents—hell, anything organic.

But those tiny, feeble deaths were too slight and exhausted quickly, leaving me hungry for more. They were a single drop of water in the desert of my thirst.

"I'll deal with that bridge when I need to burn it."

"It's been a year." He stepped back, poured himself a glass of water. The plants on the windowsill had wilted and shriveled, leaves gone brown and droopy. I wondered if he was going to fix them. Or if he, like me, parceled out how often he used the magic.

Or, rather, parceled out how often he let the magic use him.

Connections go both ways. Especially magical ones.

"We should have dealt with this months ago."

"It can wait," I said.

"No."

"But there are dead bodies out there. Magically dead bodies."

"I know. I want a promise from you, Shame."

"No more eating nachos in your bed while you're at work?"

"What?"

"What?"

He took a drink of water, and gave me that look that made me feel like I was nothing but windows from eyes to soul.

"Promise me that you will let me, once a month, do this."

"Nag me? Can we throttle that back to once a year?"

"Feed the hunger in you. The hunger in me."

"And you think that will do us any good? Really?"

He shrugged one shoulder and finished the water. "I don't know. But I'm done being in pain fighting this all the time, and you should be too. I'm calling an end to it. This is officially our thing now. Deal with it. I have an appointment. Check in on those bodies, will you?"

"Pretty sure they're still dead."

"Find out who they were. If we're going to track down the person who did this, we need to know why these people were targeted."

"Who says we're tracking down who did this?"

"I did. Just now." He walked down the hall to his bedroom and came out pulling a suit jacket on over his dress shirt.

"We're not detectives, Terric."

"You want someone else dealing with a rogue magic user? The police? And how, exactly, are they supposed to defend themselves against magic that no one should even be able to access?"

"Guns work."

"Not always."

"Please move to Canada."

He gave me a faint smile. "Find out who the victims were. We'll go from there."

"You think I'm taking orders from you?"

"See you in a few hours, Shame." He glanced over his shoulder. "There's a package coming today."

"For me?"

"No. Don't open it."

With that, he stepped out into the cool spring day.

CHAPTER 3

I sat in my car and stared at the building across the narrow street. There were a lot of people I could contact to ID the corpses. Davy and Sunny had records on every magic user who had been in the Authority, and every criminal who had not.

Other friends, like my best friends Zayvion Jones and Allie Beckstrom-Jones, would be all about helping us solve this fuck up.

But Zay and Allie had stepped away from magic and its responsibilities almost two years ago to start a family of their own.

There was no way in hell I was going to put them or my little goddaughter, Ramona Jo, at risk.

Other possible people who could handle this job included Detective Paul Stotts. He was a good cop, and had navigated the shitstorm of all the secret magic deeds coming to light with ease. He was a good magic user even though he'd never been a part of the Authority. But since he had also married Allie's best friend, Nola, I didn't want to drag him into it.

The more I thought about it, the more I decided that all my old contacts, the people I'd fought beside and fought for, the people I loved, weren't the people I should reach out to now.

They'd done their part. They'd paid their prices to keep innocent people from being hurt by magic. Some were still paying the price.

Which is what brought me here, sitting in my car across from a place I'd sworn I'd never return.

Jak's Antiques and Hardware was a crumbling brick building that might have been a firehouse back when wagons were pulled by horses. It was built alongside the Willamette River and, just like any rocky outcrop, had snagged the dregs and flotsam carried by that river for over a hundred years.

Jak had been a friend back when I was young and running hard down the wrong side of the law. I owed Jak for keeping some things quiet, and hell, for a half a dozen other things, including letting me hole up in a storage room for a month or three.

But when I'd last been here, things had gotten messy and complicated.

Seemed those two words best described my life.

I finished off my cigarette. Mostly to give myself time to think of someone—anyone—else besides Jak who might have the information I needed.

"Fuck it." I shoved on the car door and stepped out into the gusty wind coming cold off the river. "If charm don't work, bribery oughta."

I stuffed hands in my hoodie pockets and crossed the street to the side entrance of Jak's shop. The bell above the door clanged, and the smell of apple pie hit me so hard I had to swallow to keep my tongue in my mouth.

The shop was hoarder chic. Mismatched shelves groaned beneath bits and bobs that piled all the way up to the bare fluorescent lighting. Aisles—and the floor on which to walk—were more of a suggestion than a rule. Even the ceiling carried kites, model airplanes, and something that looked like a canoe tied up against it.

It would take a week with a backhoe—or maybe a few gallons of gasoline and a match—to clear this place out. But for all that it was a mess, there was a sort of organized whimsy to the joint, as if it had long ago decided to unbutton its trousers, let down its hair, and just have a good laugh at the world.

The front of the shop to my right opened up a bit for the larger pieces displayed there. A half-dozen car fenders and a stack of boxed headlights broke the monotony of the carefully arranged, free-standing glass cases that glittered with old jewelry and antique toys.

And behind a counter that looked like it had been hammered together from pieces of a barn door, was Jak.

"Shamus Flynn," Jacqueline "Jak" Hill's gritty alto called out. "You better start running before I start shooting."

"Hey, Jak. Since when do you carry a gun?"

Jak was a big woman, with soft dark skin and hair cut into short curls on the top of her head. She gave off an Aretha Franklin vibe and dressed like she belonged on stage: currently a deep ruby blouse with shiny sequin thingies glittering across the front of it. I'd found boxes of vinyl records in her basement once. She'd sung with some of the greats at an early age.

I'd asked her about it, and she'd told me it was none of my business. She never spoke of it again.

"Since when you come poking around my place?" she asked.

"Long time, right?" I asked.

"Not long enough."

Ouch.

"I probably owe you an apology."

"Probably? Boy, you owe me more than that."

"I'm good for it."

"You ain't good for nothing."

I hadn't stepped out from between the crowded aisles yet. The avalanche of dust-covered skin magazines and pinups on my left would make a decent bullet shield if she had decided to buy herself a gun. Not that I could die, exactly, but bullets hurt like a mother.

I gave her my best grin. "We both know I've always been a good for nothing. And we both know I've made mistakes. How's Claire?"

She was silent, studying me with a deep suspicion I didn't remember in her. Measured me long enough, the dust from the magazines was starting to make my nose burn.

"You stay away from her."

"I have."

"Stay away from her husband."

"Didn't even know she was married. You like him?"

"She likes him. That's good enough for me."

I nodded, waiting to see if she believed me enough not to blow my head off.

"They have kids. Two." She leaned her wide shoulders back just a bit. The chair she sat in creaked.

I strolled forward. "Really? So I should be calling you Granny Jak?"

"You should not," she chuckled. "Come here, Shame, and let me see you."

I walked to the counter, leaned my elbows on it

and waggled my eyebrows. "You want a piece of all this handsome?"

She tipped her head up as if she were looking through bifocals, even though she wasn't wearing glasses, and I saw the softening age had given her face since I'd known her.

Still, her gaze was sharp. Maybe with anger. Maybe bitter disappointment.

Her hand shot out snake-quick and fingers tipped with long, glossy, pink nails caught my chin and moved my face side-to-side.

"What have you been doing to yourself, boy?" she asked.

"Living hard."

"Mmm-hmmm," she said. "And? All that nonsense with magic I heard about?"

"Did that too." I hadn't meant for those words to come out with so much regret.

Her eyes flicked to mine, just as startled as I was at the emotion I'd bared.

"You in something you need out of?" she asked.

"No. I'm good." At her doubtful look, I added, "Now. I'm good now. Living with a guy and his boyfriend. It's..." I inhaled, exhaled. "Annoying, and crazy. Better than I deserve."

She *humphed* and let go of my chin. "That wicked

heart of yours always got you into more trouble than you deserved. You need a haircut."

I grinned and leaned back. She had told me that every day I'd known her. I didn't realize how much I'd missed it until now.

"Grandbabies, eh?"

"Boy and a girl. And another on the way."

I nodded. Tried to imagine Claire's babies with her bright brown eyes and dimples. Old sorrow shifted deep inside me, nothing but a ghost of pain from a man I could no longer be.

A man who had never been good enough to treat Claire right.

"Her husband got a name?"

"He does. Is that why you came here today? Checking up on him?"

"No. I came because I need your help."

She laughed, one loud hoot. "You have some balls, Shame Flynn. Asking me for help? After all I did for you? After all you did to us?"

"I'd understand if you tell me no."

Even. Calm. I wasn't trying to manipulate her—I'd done that enough in the past. I'd never wanted to lie to her, but that hadn't stopped me. Nor had I meant to break her heart.

"All right," she said, "then I'm saying no."

I nodded. "Well. It's been good to see you, Granny.

Take care, eh?"

I turned and waded through the aisles to the door. I'd find another way to get the records, though I had no idea how I was going to do that.

I pushed open the door.

"Hold up," she said.

I turned, one foot out, one in. "What?"

"Come here." She waved her hand over her head in a rolling motion, charm bracelets clacking and chiming. "You just going to walk out on me like that after all these years?"

"You did just tell me no. Plus, you threatened to pull a gun on me."

"That never stopped you before."

I rolled my eyes toward the ceiling. A taxidermied pig up there stared back at me. "Well, things are different now."

"And by things, you mean you?"

"Yes," I said. "And you. I'm not the one carrying a gun."

"You should be. Neighborhood's not what it used to be. None of it is what it used to be." She sounded tired of it all, and I wondered what life had done to her in the time since we'd last talked. Then she called out more gently: "Come here."

I shut the door, walked back to her counter.

"You look like a man who's seen the bottom of his

own grave, Shamus."

I tipped my head to one side in a sort of shrug. "Something like that."

"And now you're desperate enough to darken my door."

"I wouldn't say desperate."

She sniffed and raised one eyebrow. "All right. So tell me what you want my help for."

"I need some records."

"What sort?"

"IDs on a couple dead guys."

"And you think I can do that for you?"

"Yes."

"I retired from all that. Years ago. Years."

"I know."

She glanced out the window that was surprisingly whole, clean, and cornered with delicate stained glass in the shape of lilies.

"I suppose it's an important thing to bring you back here to me after all this time," she said.

"Very."

"Show me what you have." She turned back to me, her expression carefully closed down.

I pulled out my phone, opened the photos of both victims, turned the screen her way.

"This all you got? Go to the morgue. They'll run down dental records and give you what you need."

"I need more than their names. I want to know who they are, and more importantly, who they were associated with. I need to know groups, businesses, friends, family and if they had enemies or unsettled debts."

"Do I look like I work in a police department?"

"You look like you know every underground handshake deal, favor, and bribe of every cop, social worker, lawyer, insurance agent, reporter, and federal employee in the entire Pacific Northwest."

She grunted. "Not anymore. I retired." She didn't make eye contact. As a matter of fact, she was sweating even though it wasn't all that warm in the room. Was she that nervous talking to me?

Was she that afraid of me and what I'd become?

It made me wonder what she'd heard about magic. What she'd heard about me. Last I knew, word on the street was that I'd kicked some psychopath's ass for trying to kill me, my mother, and my friends. Word on the street was that the cops didn't have enough evidence to press charges against me.

Which was true, if a little light on specifics.

But Jak knew me. I didn't kill innocent people. As far as she knew, that psychopath who had nearly killed me was the only person I'd ever killed.

So why was she so nervous?

I gave her a smile. "You mean you don't go to the

races and play poker with all your old cronies? You can't kid a kidder, Jak. I know you love your vices, love your friends, and love taking their money even more."

She shook her head. "Boy, you got a long memory."

"Only for the best things in my life."

"And a candy-coated tongue." She paused again, then: "Fine. I'll find out who they are. Where were they found? When?"

She pulled a pen and a crossword puzzle book out from under the counter, and turned to a half-finished puzzle.

I gave her the streets and times, which she scribbled in the margins, her charm bracelet clacking softly against the counter with each stroke of the pen.

"How did they die?" she asked.

"Death certificates should say heart attacks."

"How did they really die, Shamus?" She lifted her pen, waited.

"I can't tell you."

"Then I can't help you." She closed the book, tucked it back under the counter.

I weighed the consequences of saying more. What were the odds any of this would get tracked back to her?

She was the cagiest researcher I had ever known. Most people didn't know about my past with her. Since she was only pulling together IDs and basic info, and she had no connection to the Authority or magic of any kind, I didn't think she would trigger any attention.

But then, I'd been wrong before.

"This is a messy thing," I said. "I don't know why they died, so I don't know who's behind it. There are too many unknowns for me to tell you more. I'm not going to put some baby's granny in danger."

She grunted. "All right. I'll let it go for now. You know I'll find out what you don't want to tell me."

"Maybe. But if you do, I want you to be quiet about it."

"Don't you go insulting me. I know more about this city than anyone. You don't see me talking."

"I know. That's one of the things I like about you. How long will it take?"

"Come back tomorrow."

"Thank you, Jak." I pressed my cool hand over the natural heat of hers. Felt the faintest brush of magic at the contact and the bitter-sweet taste of orange peels filled my mouth, which was all kinds of weird.

She jerked just slightly at my touch, but I didn't let go.

"You are a saint," I said without pause.

"I hope not. All the saints are dead." She pulled her hand away and then patted mine fondly. "Are you still messed up in all that magic business, Shame? Those people who did those terrible things?"

"The Authority is disbanded now."

"That isn't an answer."

"There isn't any magic left to be messed up in," I lied as Death magic stretched and gnawed on my insides. "No one can access it any more. All those people who used to do terrible things retired, permanently."

"I heard...things. Things you people did with magic."

"Oh?"

"If even half are half true, you should have told me what you were involved in."

"Kind of ruins the 'secret' part of 'secret organization', doesn't it?"

"I would have understood, you know. If you got tied up in things that weren't exactly legal. I would have understood that. Tried to help you."

I didn't answer for a moment. She wouldn't have understood all the things I'd done. The terrible things. She would have been angry. "Water under several bridges by now."

"Did you ever do that mind thing to me? Take my memories away?"

That mind thing was a spell known as Closing. Only a few magic users could do it. People like Terric and Zayvion. I'd never been good at it. Closing took Faith magic to fuel it and I was crap at Faith magic.

"I never have. No one has. I swear."

"And Claire?"

"And Claire."

She nodded, leaning back again to study me. "I'm taking your word on that since that's all I got."

"It's enough," I said. "It's true."

"Well," she said. "Good. Good then. Now get out of my shop. I got a game to get to."

I leaned over the counter and planted a quick kiss on her soft, warm cheek. Her perfume smelled of jasmine. Not even a hint of oranges.

She chuckled and pushed me away. "Devil."

"Saint. See you soon, Granny."

The shop door opened. A man walked in like he owned the place.

He was about my age, dressed in a button-down shirt and tie, casual jacket. Dark curly hair, dark eyes, wide, flat mouth. That flat mouth stretched into a sell-you-a-car smile that did nothing to hide the dark circles under his eyes, and something just this side of anger in his stride.

"Hey, Mom. How are you today?"

Jak went a little stiff. Or maybe I imagined it. She smiled right back—a genuine smile.

"Greg, I didn't know you'd be coming by today. Is Lolly—?"

"Fine. The same," he said a little too quickly.

Jak exhaled quietly and eased back in her chair.

"Claire wanted me to check that we were still on for dinner tonight," he said. "She's making lasagna from scratch all the way from pasta to pesto."

"Didn't I say I'd be there?"

"You know how she is," he said. "Needs to hear yes more than once."

I should have walked out. Left Jak to the family life she didn't want me involved in.

Too late. Greg nodded at me. "Hope I'm not interrupting anything."

"Not at all," I said. "Have a nice day."

I started across the shop. Didn't get very far.

"Wait," Greg said. "Is your name Flynn?"

I stopped, turned. "Have we met?"

"No." He closed the distance between us. "Greg. Greg Padgett. I think you were a friend of my wife's years ago. Claire?"

"I remember Claire," I said. "Haven't seen her in years. How is she?"

We shook. There was something in that contact, something that made me want to pull away.

Jesus. How jealous could I be? I hadn't been serious with Claire, even though she'd wanted to be serious with me. But that didn't make the instant dislike I had for the guy any easier.

"She's just great," he said. "We've got a baby on the

way." He grinned. Proud. Like the two of them had done something no one else had ever managed before.

I fixed a smile on my face. "Fantastic." I started toward the door. "Congratulations. Tell her I said hello. I wish you both the best."

"Thanks," he said. "I will."

I left the shop surprised at how quickly the old hurts and guilt with Jak and Claire had hit me.

Funny how old pain never really disappears.

I glanced at windows, roofs, street. Didn't look like I'd been followed. Even though I hadn't lied to Jak about there being no more secret magic organization, what I hadn't told her was we'd made plenty of enemies over the years.

I'd made plenty of enemies.

I wasn't a Closer like Zay, but hey, Death magic user wasn't exactly a warm-fuzzy job. I'd found ways to kill people with Death magic even before magic had been broken, then changed, the Authority had been exposed, and magic had been used, broken once more and finally locked away.

All those people who *had* been Closed now had their memories back. It wasn't a leap to think more than a few of those people wanted revenge.

Some of those people were probably on my hit list.

And if I killed them—no, when I killed them—I would make more enemies for myself.

Even twisted magical criminals had friends and family.

There were plenty of people out there who might want me dead. People who wanted to hurt the people around me.

It had happened before.

I expected it to happen again. But if there was anything I had to say about it, Jak wouldn't be caught up in it.

I owed her and Claire and what's-his-face that much, at least.

"Three babies," I muttered as I started the car and rolled down the narrow road. "Jesus, I'm getting old. Old guy needs a beer."

I turned left, toward one of my favorite pubs a few miles away.

Sun skipped through the drifting cloud cover, throwing the street into light and darkness, but no rain. No parking near the pub, so I took what I could get a couple blocks away.

This part of Portland on the East side of the river hadn't undergone gentrification yet. The warehouses, shops and houses were a comfortable collection of rust, rot, and repair. I liked it that way. It felt like home.

The passage of time, the imprint of the people who had lived and struggled here, hadn't yet been erased beneath the preservative glass globe of wealth.

The sidewalk gave way to mud and gravel. I tromped through that, dug in my coat for a cigarette.

Sunlight dipped, sending the world into gray, then popped hard again, too bright, too gold, the wind kicking a sudden gust.

I lowered my head and turned sideways away from the wind to light my smoke.

Pain stabbed through my shoulder, riding the crack of gunshot.

"Fuck." I ducked behind a parked car, grabbing at my bleeding shoulder. The ricochet of three more bullets rattled through the air.

No one on the street. No one in the parked cars. Down the block, the door to the pub opened, letting out the sound of the Timber's game.

One of the bartenders, a phone pressed to his ear, looked up and down the street, then pulled back into the bar.

Calling 911. I did my own surveillance. Plenty of places to hide the shooter across the street in, on top of, or between the half-abandoned buildings.

Shit.

I took the last drag off my cigarette, leaned up against the car and dragged Death magic up from my bones, casting it out like a net around me.

Heartbeats. Loud as drums. Each beat a pulse against my pulse. Hot and slick, all the lives, all that living, spread out like food, like sex, like pleasure so carnal, I moaned.

I pushed the hunger aside. Ignored the need. Focused on the hearts. Human hearts, not the finger-drumming rattle of rodents and birds, cats and dogs. Just the humans. Just this street.

Thirty in the pub, one dying of cancer, another weak from surgery. A few in the upper floor on my side of the street, sleeping. Seven at the end of the block sweating in a garage. Ten across the street—maybe an office—worried, hearts elevated. And that one slow steady throb, a heart pushing down adrenalin, too calm for the hormones rushing through veins.

My shooter was a pro. Lousy shot, but still, a pro.

I could kill him with Death magic, but only if I could put my hands on him. That was one of the drawbacks to locking magic away. It had changed the rules for how it could be used.

The rattle of hard wheels over concrete turned my attention to the right. A couple of kids, boys, neither over eight, pushed this way on a skateboard and scooter. Maybe excited to see what all the shooting was about.

Shit. If Crap Shot up there on the third floor of the building across the street popped off a few and missed, he'd hit those kids.

I stood, stared at a crack in the window behind which I knew my shooter was crouched.

Had no idea if he was still reloading, but no one headed out to kill a person packing only one round.

The kids rolled down the street, oblivious as only kids can be.

Dammit.

I stepped out from behind the car and strode across the street. Not away from the bullets. Right into them.

He squeezed off another two shots, only one hit— same damn shoulder. I got my swearing on, clenched my teeth through the pain.

Fucking bastard.

If he wanted me dead, he sure was taking the long damn road to it.

Sirens squalled on the edge of my hearing, grew louder fast.

The kids scattered.

The gunman was in a hurry to pack it up. I could taste his fear.

I made the opposite sidewalk, jogged the wooden stair attached to the side of the building.

Bones were going to break—a lot of them, and none of them mine—before I killed the bastard.

Door at the top of the stairs was padlocked. Braced on the inside.

I pressed both palms against the wood near the handle and lock. Death magic sucked the strength out of it, drinking and aging the wood down to rot and dust.

I kicked open the damn door.

Storage room filled with cardboard boxes. Stank of film chemicals. A broken cardboard box was spread flat in front of the crack in the window that looked out over the street.

No gunman. No trace of gunman.

Fuck it all to hell.

The window on the other side of the room was open. I strode over there, leaned out. Didn't see him. Didn't feel him.

The sirens were close now. Unless I wanted them to find me in the middle of the crime scene, it was time to move.

I scanned the room with eyes and Death magic.

Got a ping. By the window where the shooter had tried to blow my head off, lay a broken stick thick as my middle finger and about as long.

There was something magical about it.

I picked it up.

All my instincts told me to take it. It didn't look magical. Looked like a stick.

Screw it. I shoved the stick in my pocket.

I snarled at the throbbing pain in my shoulder. Left the room. Jogged down the stairs and across the block.

Slipped into my car as two police cruisers rounded the corner. They stopped outside the pub.

I didn't stay to see what happened.

Drove home, angry. Tossed the stick in the cup holder to deal with it later.

I had no idea who had been taking shots at me.

Too damn many people wanted me dead, and the only clue I had were the bullets in my arm.

I pushed out of the car, slammed the door, still swearing. The pain in my shoulder was starting to soak through the protective barrier of my rage.

Terric pulled up in the driveway, killed the engine and got out of the car. "What's wrong?"

"Nothing." I stormed into the house. Left the door open for him even though I was feeling the need to slam something.

"Did the package arrive?" He closed the door gently and hung his jacket while I continued my march down to my room.

"How the fuck should I know? I just got here."

"Are you bleeding?" His tone changed. "Why are you bleeding?"

I yanked open my bedroom door and stopped cold on the threshold.

A woman, probably in her twenties, lay on top of my bed, a maroon hoodie tossed over her slim hips for a blanket. Her short shag of honey brown hair was tossed over her sleep-glossed eyes, elbow propped so she could stare at me.

CHAPTER 4

"Terric," I said, both pain and anger temporarily forgotten. "You shouldn't have."

He stepped up behind me, glanced into the room over my shoulder.

"Jolie?" he said.

"Who?"

"My sister, Jolie." He pushed me aside. "What are you doing here?"

"In my room," I added, "not that I mind you, looking like that, in my bed…"

"Sister, Shame," Terric said.

"Hey." Jolie sat up the rest of the way. She had on a worn-out gray T-shirt, with what was either a high school mascot or a pizza stain down the front of it, jeans and boots. "Sorry. Long bus ride."

Terric helped her to the edge of the bed like she

was fragile. But that look she was giving me wasn't fragile at all.

"Really, Ter," I said. "I'm good with the naughty Sleeping Beauty thing she's got going there."

"Aw." She flicked me a grin. "Beauty? Last time you saw me, you called me brat."

"We've met?" I tried to place her in my memories of the mob of brothers, sisters, and cousins that had always surrounded my visits to Terric's parents' place when we were younger.

Terric exhaled loudly. "Of course you've met. We were fifteen."

I studied the woman in front of me. All her curves and edges, and that specific curve of her bottom lip that had a tiny white scar right below the center of it. Either an accident, or she'd pierced it.

She was younger than me. By more than a couple years.

I dredged my mind for the vague images of Terric's younger sisters, trying to place her among the pigtails, torn-jean knees, braces, and freckles of my memories.

Jolie bit her bottom lip, straight white teeth pressing into her pink softness in a move that was all woman. The corner of that mouth tipped a cat-like smile.

"Don't you remember me, Shaney?"

"First: that nickname? Not going to happen. And no, I don't remember. How old were you?"

"Ten."

"Jesus. Ten?" I looked her up and down.

She stood and shrugged back into the hoodie, the T-shirt hiking up to bare a palm width of pale skin across her flat stomach and hip as she did so.

The edge of a tattoo along her left hipbone peeked over the low waist of her jeans.

Mercy.

"I've grown up a little," she said.

"Yeah, you have," I said with maybe a little too much heat.

"Shame," Terric warned. Then, "Jolie, why are you here? I thought you were in college."

"Right. About that." She turned those blue eyes— deeper blue than Terric's—toward her brother. "Things got...weird. I left."

"College?"

"College. Town. Everything. Since you asked for my help..."

"I called to check in on you. I didn't ask for your help."

"...I decided to deliver the package myself."

"What package?" I asked.

"Some things I needed from Mom and Dad's storage," Terric said.

"Baby photos?"

"Designs from my closed business up in Seattle. Nothing," he said, turning to Jolie, "that couldn't have been mailed to me. Mailed."

"Yeah, well, you get the personal touch." Jolie picked up the messenger bag on the floor next to the bed and drew a large manila file out of it. "I have the tube in my suitcase."

"You're going home," he said.

"No, I'm not. I'm..." She bit her lip again. Not in a sexy way. She was afraid. "I'm in trouble, Terric. I need your help."

Terric stood there a moment, studying her. I could feel a faint hint of his emotions, stirred up by her being here and saying those words. Anger and distrust, but overwhelming those was his worry and love for her.

"What kind of trouble?" he finally asked.

"Tell you over a cup of coffee and some toast? I'm starving."

He seemed to remember we were all standing in my bedroom. Nodded.

"Fine. Kitchen's down the hall."

I moved out of the doorway so Jolie could walk by. Caught the faintest hint of her perfume. Liked it.

"Nice place," she said. "Not what I expected out of you, though, Terric."

"It's Shame's house."

"Oh. That explains it."

Terric hadn't stopped frowning. He walked to my door, eyes on his sister as she walked down the hall.

"She shouldn't be around us right now," I said, crossing to my dresser.

"I know," he said, distracted. He rubbed at his shoulder absently. "Why are you hurting?"

"Took a couple in the arm today."

He finally looked over at me. "A couple what? Fists?"

"Bullets."

That wiped all the unfocused out of his eyes. "God damn it, Shame. Why didn't you tell me?"

"I just did." I pulled off my hoodie and hissed when the fabric yanked out of the holes in my arm.

"Let me see."

I knew better than to argue with him. When Terric got it in his mind to heal something—anything—there was no stopping him. None.

I'd tried. It had never ended well.

I pushed my bloody T-shirt sleeve away from my bloody arm.

"Who shot you?" He placed one hand on the back of my arm. Cool numbing spread under his touch as if he'd just dipped my biceps in Novocain.

I couldn't hold back the sigh of relief.

The lack of pain came with a lack of adrenalin. I

fought down exhaustion because I was not about to pass out at Terric's feet.

"I don't know," I said.

"You must have some idea." He placed the palm of his other hand gently over the entry wounds. This numbness came with healing warmth.

It was nice. Real nice.

"Shame?" he said quietly.

I knew he was pulling on magic. Using it to heal me. Life magic. I knew Life magic pushed him to do this, and letting him heal was actually a favor to him.

But our past—the things we'd done with magic—and more than that, the things magic had done to us, made me want to pull away.

I didn't want my need for life to hurt him.

"What?" I asked.

"I got this. I got you. Stop pushing."

I frowned. "What?"

"You know."

I glanced down at his hand on my arm.

Blood pooled between his closed fingers, then was gone. In a moment, it pooled there again.

The Death magic in me was unhealing his healing: drinking Life magic, re-opening the wound so he could heal it again and I could drink down the life again.

"Shit." I punched down on the Death magic inside

me, pushing it like a huge, unruly snarl of pain and hunger into the closet of my control.

"Better," Terric said. He pressed more firmly on the front of my arm, then drew away his hand from the back. I heard the clack of two small metal slugs in his hand.

"How bad?" I asked.

"Without me? You'd lose some use of the hand." He dropped the bullets in my palm.

"With you?"

"Full recovery."

And there it was. The reason why Terric wanted to keep Life magic in his body, even though there were drawbacks.

"Are you sure you don't know who plugged you?" he asked.

"Didn't get a read on him. A man. That's it before the cops showed up."

"Did they see you?"

"No."

"Good. Clean up. I don't want Jolie asking questions."

"You going to let go of my arm?"

"Oh." He stepped back, and for a very uncharacteristic moment, looked embarrassed. Him healing me was good for him too.

"We'll be in the kitchen," he said.

"Got it. Thanks, Doc."

He gave me a nod. "We don't tell her about this, right?"

"Hell yes, right," I said. "We don't let her live here either, right?"

"Live here? Not a chance."

"Good. People like to shoot at us."

"Us?"

"Me. Which means anyone around me is in danger of getting shot at. And I'm not going to be the cause of your little sister finding out what lead under the skin feels like."

"You'll get no argument from me. We'll send her home on the first train or plane out tomorrow."

He stepped out.

I tossed the bullets in my sock drawer with the other slugs I'd picked up over the last year. I dragged off my T-shirt, wadded it up, and threw it in the bathroom hamper. Scrubbed the blood off my arm and hand in the sink, then took a look at myself.

Green eyes still too dark, skin paper white, needed a shave. Hair was getting a little out of control. Jak was right. It could use a cut.

I smiled and shook my head. The smile did a lot to spread some humanity into the bones and edges of my face, into my eyes.

I might not be only human anymore since I carried

magic in me as sure as blood and breath, but I was at least still human-adjacent.

Good enough.

Pulled on a new T-shirt—plain black just like the last—strolled out into the hall, then down to the kitchen.

CHAPTER 5

Terric and Jolie were talking quietly.

The fresh, deep smell of coffee brewing rolled over my senses and drew me on.

"Hacking?" Terric asked.

Jolie sat at the small table, three pieces of buttered toast stacked on the plate in front of her. Terric leaned against the counter by the coffeepot.

I opened the fridge, pulled out the homemade apricot jam my mother had given me a week ago. It was packaged with a fancy hand-crafted label. She was selling her homemade jams out of her restaurant and inn, and apparently couldn't keep it on the shelf.

"Some hacking," Jolie said. "Nothing illegal."

"All hacking is illegal."

"If you hack for the Feds it's not," she said.

I set the jam on the table in front of her. "Were you hacking for the Feds?"

She rolled her eyes. "No."

"Who, Jolie?" Terric asked.

She tipped her head down and shoved toast in her mouth. "The Russians."

"The Russian what?" Terric asked.

"Mob."

I whistled, and Terric cussed. "The fuck, Jolie? You're hacking for the Russian mob?"

"Not anymore, duh."

"Do. Not," Terric snapped.

Jolie studied him, glanced at me.

"He is pissed as hell at you right now," I provided helpfully, crossing my arms over my chest.

Her eyebrows dipped and her gaze measured both of us. Out of the corner of my eye, Terric stood as a mirror reflection to me: arms crossed over his chest, feet spread.

Jesus. This connection between us had crept into everything we did.

I turned to the cupboard and drew out mugs.

"Explain." Terric growled. When that man devolved down to one-word demands, he was more than pissed.

The dead plants on the windowsill stirred as if a

breeze had just blasted through the room. Which it hadn't. He was letting Life magic slip.

That wasn't good. That was never good.

Jolie glanced that way, startled.

"Leaky seal around the window," I said. "I told you to fix that, Terric."

He turned his gaze on me, and there was anger and magic burning there.

"That leaky window is really doing a job on those plants," I said, pushing those words, and the intent behind them, through our connection and into his thick, angry, magic-muddled head.

"Window?" he asked.

I picked up his hand and used it to point at the window. I also sent a snap of Death magic at him.

"That window."

"Ow. Oh," he said. "Right. I'll take care of it."

He drew Life magic back under control and the plants stopped moving.

"So how deep is this shit pit you've dug yourself into?" I asked Jolie as I poured coffee.

"Deep." She put her toast down and looked a little sick.

I offered her the coffee. Her hand shook as she took it.

"It would be best to be really, really clear about it," I said. "We promise to hear you out. Won't we, Terric?"

I stuck a coffee mug against his chest and stood so I was blocking his view of his sister.

Ice-blue eyes ticked down to me. I raised an eyebrow. "We're going to listen to the situation your sister got herself into and see if we can't get her out of it, right?"

His mouth did that sour lemon thing.

"The mob," he repeated.

"People make mistakes."

"Not with the mob."

"The mob are people, too."

His nostrils flared, but he nodded shortly. "Out of the way, Shame."

I dipped my head and stepped aside. He took the coffee out of my hand and sat at the table across from Jolie.

I gave her a wink from behind Terric's back.

She still looked a little green: pink patches of heat on her cheeks and pale everywhere else.

She was scared. Terrified.

"Just take it slow and walk us through it," I said over Mr. Brood and Silent's head.

I leaned on the counter behind Terric and thought calm thoughts, because, hell, one of us ought to.

"I met this girl," she started. "She was making money doing some computer work for a guy who was trying to get his business up and running."

"Business?" I asked.

"Records. Vinyl, 8-tracks. Hipster shit."

"Go on."

"She said there was more work than she could handle. Offered to hook me up. I started working for him. Building basic inventory systems, tracking software. Stuff like that. He bought and sold in practically every country, so there were taxes, money conversions, and a lot of paperwork. It was a pretty big job for a start-up that didn't even have a name or an outlet store. He did own a shitload of warehouses. All over the world."

"Guns, drugs, or human trafficking?" I asked.

Her eyes ticked to the left for a moment. She was either lying, or didn't like what she was about to tell me.

"All three, I think. I jumped ship as soon as I found proof that guns and drugs were involved."

"Jumped ship?" I asked.

She gulped down some coffee, stared into her cup. From this angle, I could see the frightened ten-year-old in her. But when her gaze pulled up to meet mine, she was not a frightened girl. She was a woman who intended to survive.

"I re-appropriated their funds."

I tipped my head as if I hadn't heard her. "Excuse me? You stole from the mob?"

"No. I funneled their funds into charitable organizations. A...lot of charitable organizations."

"Hoo-lee shit." I laughed. "What happens if the charitable organizations track where all that money is coming from?"

She shrugged. "It wouldn't be hard to find the link. And then...well, some of the organizations would probably go to the police. Or the Feds."

"How much money?" Terric-the-Silent finally asked.

"A lot. Like...a *lot*."

"Do the Russians know you did it?" I asked.

"I didn't stay to find out."

I sucked air in through my teeth. "Ouch."

"What?" she asked.

"It would have been better if you had stayed," Terric said.

"Except I'd be dead by now."

"Have you seen that kind of activity out of them?" I asked.

She tipped her eyes down again, drank coffee. "Megan's missing."

"Who?"

"My friend who got me the job."

"And you think she's dead?" Terric asked. "Jolie, do you have proof? College kids run off, drop out every day."

"I don't think she bailed. I think she's...gone. And like you said, college kids drop out of sight all the time. Maybe the Russians will think that's what I did."

"You wouldn't be here if you believed that," I said.

"You still have contacts, don't you?" she said to Terric. "All those years you worked for the Authority, you must have met people who can deal with this stuff."

"Why do you think I worked for the Authority for years?"

"I'm curious. And smart. And quiet. People tend to ignore me. Especially when I was younger. So, I did some digging."

"How long have you known?" he asked.

"I figured it out when I was nine. You suddenly went away to go to school in Portland with some old man who said he'd take you in as a private student. I never believed you went off to learn graphic design."

"I did, actually."

That was the time I'd first met Terric. We'd both been about fourteen when we'd started training with Victor and the Authority, along with Zayvion and several others.

"But it wasn't all you learned from that man," she said.

"No." He shook his head once. "But you know that no one can use magic like we did...before..."

"Before?"

"Before the Authority went public with all the secret magic it was hiding," I added over the top of my mug. "Before magic got shut down for good."

"About that," she said. "I've done a little digging into why magic isn't accessible to everyone any more. Why it doesn't work. Why it suddenly stopped working."

"And?" I asked.

"Maybe you have a theory I should know about?" she asked.

"Global warming?"

She rolled her eyes.

Terric and I hadn't told anyone we were to blame for locking magic up. I might be Death; but I'm not suicidal.

"How should I know?" I said. "Maybe magic just turns off every so many hundred years. It's not like anyone has kept good records on it."

"Except maybe the Authority?" she said.

No wonder she'd found out about the Authority when she was nine. She was more than curious, she was tenacious. That was a dangerous and, I admitted, an intriguing combination to be all wrapped up in her mostly-innocent looking package.

"If the Authority had records on that," I said, dead serious, "we haven't seen them. No one's seen them.

Not even the intelligence agencies that swooped down on the Authority's twitching corpse and tore it apart, data bit by data bit."

"You don't think someone in the Authority destroyed the records before the intelligence agencies got there, do you?"

"They were magic users," Terric said quietly. "If they wanted something, anything, or anyone gone—that's what happened. No matter the cost."

"But you still have contacts, right?" she said. "People you could talk to. People who could help me disappear?"

"Jesus, Jolie," Terric said. "You're not going to disappear."

"Aren't I? I knew what I was doing, Terric. I knew how much it would piss them off. And unless you're going to take on the entire Russian mob, big brother, I don't see any other way out of this."

"There's always a way out," he said.

"I'm open for suggestions."

"I don't have one. Yet. Until we figure it out, you're staying here with us."

I choked on my coffee. Was pretty sure we'd just decided the opposite of that.

"Really?" she said, all hopeful eyes and fast heartbeat.

"Of course, really."

Looking at her, at that hope, I felt like a total heel for wanting to send her back home, send her far, far away from us and the current mess we were in.

"Terric?" I said. "A word?" I walked out of the kitchen. "What happened to ten minutes ago? Where we decided there was no way we were going to let her live in this very dangerous house?"

"Where else is she supposed to go?" he angry-whispered. "Who else but you and I can keep her safe?"

"Keep her safe while we deal with someone killing with magic?" I asked. "If that goes to hell and we don't find out who's doing that, the Russian mob's going to look like fuzzy duckies compared to the fight we're headed into."

"I know."

"Someone is killing people with magic," I reminded him, as he had reminded me just a few hours ago. "Killing."

He inhaled, exhaled, his worry and pain churning between us. "What do you want me to do, Shame? Where can we send her so she'll be safe?"

I thought about the basement storage under Jak's shop and knew even that wouldn't keep her away from the mob for long. There wasn't any place I could think of where she'd be safe.

"Fuck."

"Exactly," he said.

"So, we what? Kill a few high-powered members of the mob? Let them know snuffing a few of their guys meant they got off easy? Tell them if they try to touch her, we'll tear them apart nuts to nails?"

"We can't just meet them in an alley with guns," he said.

"We wouldn't need guns."

"Then how would you kill them?" Jolie asked from where she was leaning on the doorway to the hall.

Terric stiffened, his gaze shooting up over my shoulder.

I turned so I could see her. "Really? How does you listening in on our private conversation in *my* house work?"

"I didn't think it was that private."

"We were whispering."

"But you weren't behind closed doors."

"Terric, I'm going to throttle your sister."

"Take a number, Flynn."

The front door opened.

Terric and I shifted toward it. Jolie pressed against the wall, smaller than the shadow in the hall.

CHAPTER 6

"We've got another dead guy," Dash said, back toward us as he kicked the door closed. "Same as the other two. Death by magi—" He spun our way, a pizza box in his hands. Took in Terric, me. Looked behind us, found Jolie.

"—it's not a good time, is it?" he said.

"Never a bad time for pizza," I said.

Jolie eased out from the shadows and stood there, one hand clasped against her elbow.

"Dash," Terric said, "this is—"

"Your sister, Jolie." Dash finished for him.

"Yes," Terric said, confused. "How did you know?"

"You had pictures of your family on your walls at your old place. You named them all off to me once."

"Three years ago?"

He shrugged. "I have a good memory. Also, I see

the family resemblance." He handed Jolie the pizza box. "Hey. I'm Dash. Nice to meet you. Hope you like pepperoni."

"Who doesn't?"

"We'll be at the table in a minute," Terric said.

She feigned surprise. "Oh? I'm supposed to sit in the kitchen while you all talk about the dead guy and magic, right?"

"You came here for our help," Terric said. "Stop getting in the way of us trying to do that."

"Sure," she said. "I'll just eat pizza while the men solve my problems."

"Sarcasm," I said. "I like it. As soon as we men figure out what resources we can throw at your problems, you'll get a vote on how those resources are used. And no, we're not going to let you in on our talk. Just because you think you know what's been going on in our lives for the last decade doesn't mean you do."

"Well, I can't help you help me if I don't know what's going on."

"Sorry," I said. "Those are ground rules, Jolie. You're family. But that doesn't give you the right to use us any way you see fit."

Her cheeks went a high color and her chin tipped up, eyes flashing dangerously. Every inch of her radiated the need to yell.

I waited for it. For her to scream about how unfair

her life was, because, yes, I sympathized. Life wasn't fair. It wasn't fair that we would have to make some decision about her life without her.

"I'm not a child," she said evenly.

"I know. Believe me, I know. You got this far on your own, kept your head above water. I respect the hell out of you for that. But you need to give us a few minutes to lower the lifeboat before you start shooting holes in it, okay?"

"Better be beer in the lifeboat," she muttered.

I grinned. "Might manage a Bud."

"Rogue Ale, or don't bother rowing home."

She had good taste.

"I'll see what I can do."

She walked off into the kitchen, shoulders straight, head held high.

Woman was full of determination.

"Don't know that I appreciate your tone with my little sister, Shame," Terric said. "Or how you're looking at her."

"I'm not looking at her."

"You remember we're connected? I know exactly how you're looking at her."

"Outside, gentlemen?" Dash suggested.

We took it outside. Closed the door and stood over by the cars, where it would be practically impossible for Jolie to hear us.

"Why is your sister here?" Dash asked.

"She got herself mixed up with the Russian mob."

"Oh, hell."

Terric nodded.

"How bad?"

"Well," Terric said, "the best plan we have so far is to go kill a few people until they understand they need to back off."

"Is negotiation out of the question?"

"Don't think they'll want to talk." I lit a cig, took a puff. "She funneled a crapload of their money into charity organizations."

Dash grinned and ran his fingers back through thick hair. "You Conleys like to poke bears with sticks, don't you?"

"She got tangled up in their business routing international drug and gun deals," Terric said. "Bailed with her middle fingers flying."

"Okay," he said. "Who are we going to kill? And how is that not going to make her more of a target?"

"We haven't figured that part out yet," I said. "Terric and I could take a trip up to Seattle. Kick over some hives."

"That will take too long and leave a messy trail," he said.

"True," I said.

"She knows who she was working for," Dash said.

"Let's get that info out of her, track it back to the boss's boss, or however high up we have to go. Set up a meeting. Explain that we want this handled without bloodshed. Explain why it's in their best interests to leave her alone before all the blood that gets shed is theirs."

I sucked on the cigarette, considering it. My usual gut response to threat was to hit back hard, but Dash's way might be better.

"Russians aren't going to believe us without proof of what we can do to them," Terric said.

"So, you prove it to them," Dash said. "That's where the meeting comes in."

"Prove, as in: kill them with magic?" I asked. "I'd rather not let the Russian mob in on that little secret."

"You don't have to show them how you kill. Just that you're more than willing to do it. Maybe to someone they care about."

"You have a dark streak, you know that, Dash?"

"It's not like this is my first roller derby."

"True. Terric?"

"It makes sense. Let's ask her what she knows. Find out who we can lean on, set up a meeting. Did you find anything on the IDs of our magically dead, Shame?"

"I have someone working on it. Should have something by tomorrow," I said. "What about you, Dash? You found a fresh corpse?"

"Already down at the morgue by now. Middle-aged

white guy. Found in an alley. Magic burns on his chest, face, neck."

"Shit," I said.

"Who found him?" Terric asked. "Where? When?"

"Some kids. He was in an alley behind the bar down on Third, this morning."

"Did you get pictures?" Terric asked.

"No. Police were on the scene. I tried to snap something on my way into the pizza place next door, but couldn't get a clear shot."

"Did you recognize him?" I asked.

He shook his head.

"Someone needs to go wipe the magic marks off of him," I said.

"Police already saw it," Dash said. "There's no changing that."

"Someone needs to ID him," Terric said.

"They probably already have," I said.

"So we wait?" Dash asked.

"I hate waiting," I said.

"Okay." Terric stared off in the distance and tucked his hands into his pockets, the breeze stirring the edges of his short, white hair.

I watched Dash watch him with steady eyes. Wondered why the two of them were arguing over the job offer in Canada. Wondered if it was something more—the flame of the relationship burning out. But no, from the look on Dash's face, he still cared for Terric. Loved him.

"Shame," Terric said, "you and Dash go down to the morgue, see if you can slip in and get a first-hand look at the guy and the glyphs. Chances that the police will actually reveal the cause of death are slim-to-none. We're going to make sure it looks like magic wasn't the thing that killed him, that it was something else. We're going to make sure the magical marks look like they were carved into his skin as an afterthought."

"We're covering the tracks of a serial killer by making him look like a serial killer?" I asked.

"We're keeping the magical component out of these deaths. Until we find out who the hell is doing this and how the hell they're accessing magic to do it."

There was a reason Terric was given the job of running the Authority. He was a natural leader.

"All right. Fine," I said. "Are you going to talk to your sister about all this?"

"Enough of it. What she needs to know. And I'll get the information on her contacts. We'll decide who to contact, and how, when you get back from the morgue."

"Corpse molestation. And here I didn't think the day could get any worse than getting shot."

"You got shot?" Dash asked.

"I'll fill you in on the drive." I tossed the cigarette and strode over to my car.

I gave Dash and Terric an awkward moment to decide if they were going to talk. When all they did was sort of stare at each other, I rapped knuckles on the car hood.

"Dash. Dead guy isn't getting any deader. Let's go."

Dash mumbled something to Terric, eyes on his boots.

I didn't have to look at Terric to feel the mess of emotions Dash had just stirred in him.

Terric nodded slightly.

Dash strode to the car, got in. "Someone shot you? Again?"

"It's been a delightful morning." Then, as Terric walked past my window: "There better be pizza left when I get home."

Terric ignored me and walked into the house.

CHAPTER 7

My mum told me to work hard. Insisted that if I did, I'd make a good life for myself. But all my hard work had gotten me dead, tortured, re-dead, kicked out of heaven, re-alived, and now squatting in the bushes behind a morgue.

"It's called breaking and entering, Dash, not gently picking the damn lock for an hour."

He shifted to get a better angle on the window lock. "Shut up and keep an eye out."

"No one's coming. Doesn't take my eyes for that. There's dead in the basement and all three of the living are in the upstairs lunch room. Except for the one guy who's out pissing on someone's grave north-ish of here, we're alone. Alone enough, I don't know why we don't go through the open front doors."

"Cameras. We don't have magic to turn them off any more, Shame. You know that."

I sighed, stared at the bellies of clouds gone gray with rain. I did miss the easy tricks we used to have in a world more magical.

"He wants you to stay," I said.

"What?"

"Terric. I know he told you to take the job, but he wants you to stay."

"Jesus. Haven't you heard of privacy and none-of-your business?"

"Yes and yes. He only told you to go because he thinks you want to. He thinks it will be a good career move for you."

Dash paused, his hands steady on the lock picks while he gave me a hard stare. "If that's what he thinks, he can tell me that. Not you. Got it?"

"Got it," I agreed. "But one of you is going to have to call a truce before neither of you gets what you want out of this standoff."

He grunted. "Just like one of you called a truce with the whole Life/Death magic connection?"

Huh. I hadn't thought my connection to Terric was a problem for Dash. Maybe the old pain of the old shit we'd done to each other was something Dash still carried around.

I should probably just respect his space. Keep my mouth shut. Make his business none of mine.

But what would be the fun of that?

"Jealous of what we have, mate?"

He stopped again, this time pivoting in his crouch to fully face me. "You mean that connection that you hate, Shame? Soul-to-soul, so you feel every damn thing the other is feeling? That thing that Terric says he doesn't want but can't live without? Can't leave this town without? Is that the thing you want to know if I'm jealous about?"

"Well, not anymore."

I wondered for a moment if he was going to stab me with the lock pick, but he turned and stabbed the lock instead. "It's not...it's not that," he said, all anger out of his voice. "Terric's my boyfriend, but you...well, you're like the dog we adopted together."

"Whoa. Better back up, mate."

"Surly, messy. Growl a lot. Bite. Don't bathe enough."

"I bathed. Recently."

"But you are something...you are *someone* we both care for. Someone we both can't see living our lives without. So. No. I'm not jealous of your connection. I just wish he'd tell me...."

He inhaled, exhaled. "I'm not going to gripe about my relationship issues with you, Shame."

"Fair," I said. "Then might I suggest you tell him all these things you're almost telling me? Just tell him you want him to tell you not to go. That you want him to tell you he loves you and can't live without you."

That stilled him—hands, body, breath. Only his heartbeat was racing.

"You sure think you know how people work for someone who doesn't give a damn."

"Well, what does that tell you? Jesus. Give me the picks. I think that lock's a girl. You have no idea how to open one up."

Dash choked on a laugh, rocked back on his heels, and shook his head. "And now you think you're funny."

"I think I'm hilarious. Gimme." I grabbed for the lock picks. He slapped them into my palm and moved out of the way so I could get to the lock.

"All right," I said, cupping the picks and making a fist around them.

I punched out the lowest square of the windowpane.

"Fuck, Shame."

Stuck my hand through and turned the lock from the inside. "There we go, you naughty girl. Daddy knows you like it rough."

"Daddy better hurry up," Dash said. "They probably have alarms on the windows, you ass. That's why we brought the picks."

"Details." I pulled on the window. The bottom half of it slid up, leaving an open space big enough for Dash and me to scramble through. I went first.

Short drop onto concrete floor. Long, dark room. But the darkness could not hide the smell of death, the awareness of the dead that brushed beneath my skin like a cool breeze.

It was both uncomfortable and soothing. So I did my best to ignore it.

Dash dropped down behind me. Clicked something. A flashlight.

"Boy Scout," I said.

He handed me another flashlight. "Eagle, actually. Can you tell which drawer he's in?"

I flicked on the flashlight and strolled over to the wall of four drawers. Only two of them were occupied. One by a woman. One by a guy killed by magic.

I tapped on the drawer. "Want another shot at the lock?"

"Can you do it fast? Without your fist?"

I rolled the lock picks into my fingers and handed him the flashlight. "Let's find out, shall we?"

He leveled the light, and I jimmied the lock. Got it sprung in ten seconds. "Look who gets his lock picking badge."

"It only counts if we don't get caught, Tiger Scout."

I took the flashlight, tugged the drawer, rolling it open.

Body bag. Zipped shut. Tag said John Doe.

"Maybe the cops haven't ID'ed him yet." I unzipped the bag, stared down at the guy. "Shit."

Dash stood on the other side of the drawer. "That's messy."

It took me a second to register what Dash had said.

He was right. This guy had been killed with magic, the same three glyphs: Pain, Binding, Surrender. But our killer was a lot sloppier about it. The glyphs were burned into his eyes, burrowed into one side of his face, and slashed across his throat like a dull saw blade had done the work.

But that wasn't what had stopped me cold.

"I know him."

"Who is he?"

"Lyle Carpenter."

Dash shook his head. "Friend?"

"Acquaintance of an acquaintance of my mum's. Decent man."

"Ah. Sorry, Shame."

"Notice the ink?" I pointed toward his chest.

It was a fish, maybe a Koi, tail curled down across his ribs, body curved over his heart.

"Think it's the same as your guy?" he asked.

"Might be."

I unzipped the body bag the rest of the way and studied his skin, looking for other marks, other signs of the asshole who had done this. Nothing. Just those sloppy, untrained glyphs.

"Was he part of the Authority?" Dash asked.

"No. Not that I knew of. He wasn't even a casual magic user. Ran a real estate office out on the TV Highway."

"Why use magic to kill a real estate agent?"

"Fuck if I know. Do you smell oranges?"

He took a tentative sniff. "No. I smell chemicals and dead flesh."

I zipped the bag back up to his chest and pressed my palm over his forehead. The cold meat gave way with a sort of squish beneath the gentle pressure.

I sent Death magic into the decaying organic matter, through flesh and bone, and urged the remaining matter to form a clot in the veins. It was tedious, sweaty work, like pressing clay that had gone too dry into shape while it crumbled in my hands.

Finally pulled away.

"What did you do?"

"Aneurism. Pretty sure. Or tumor, or blockage. Something that will explain his death if they go all out for an autopsy."

"What about the glyphs?"

"Getting there."

I stuck two fingers against the middle of his fore-head like some kind of holy man giving last rites. But this wasn't a blessing.

I tipped my head and closed my eyes. I wanted to know how magic had been used to kill him.

The magic that clung to these glyphs wasn't like any I'd felt before. This magic felt like a hot blade, acid that couldn't be handled, shouldn't be touched.

This magic wasn't power and potential that could be guided to take shape and action.

This was an atomic reaction that consumed every-thing it touched.

How had someone manipulated something like that? How had they contained it with such poorly drawn glyphs?

There might be a reason why the glyphs were drawn so poorly. Either whoever was casting them was in immense pain while doing so, or...

Or what?

Or we'd just found someone who had discovered how to wield magic that no one should be able to use as an executioner's blade.

There were a hundred easier ways to kill a man. Breaking magic out of the locks we'd put on it should take enormous effort.

And why kill these men? What did they have in common? Who the hell had they all pissed off?

I drew the residue of magic out of the burns. As carefully as I could, I changed the glyph wounds so they were just magic-less burns.

Looked like someone had done a shit job with a branding iron.

I stepped back, swallowed against the sick taste in my mouth.

"There is something wrong here," I said.

"What gave you that idea?" Dash asked. "The dead guy?"

I flipped him the finger. "Snap a couple pictures and let's get the hell out of here."

Dash snapped; I zipped the bag back over Lyle. We wiped our prints off every surface, shut the drawer, cleaned the handle, then reset the lock.

We scrambled up out the window. I closed it behind us, took time to wipe it down, gave the frame one last brush.

"They'll know someone broke in, since it's broken," Dash said as we pushed out of the shrubs and strolled to the car.

"Someone, but not us," I said. "Let's get home. It's time for our ex-Russian vigilante hacker to help us track down a killer."

CHAPTER 8

"No," Terric whispered, his back against my closed bedroom door. "My sister is not going to hack, track, or get involved in the magic deaths."

I sat on the edge of my bed. The faint honey and cinnamon of Jolie's perfume clung to the blankets. Nice. Distracting.

"She took on the Russians," I said. "Found a way to funnel their money into charities. That's out-of-the-box thinking. We need that right now."

"No. She doesn't know anything about the magic...about us."

I knew he meant she didn't know we carried magic, didn't know we had been the ones who were responsible for locking it away.

"It was Lyle Carpenter," I said.

"Who?"

"Realtor. My mum pointed him out once or twice when he stopped by the inn."

"Part of the Authority?"

"Not that I know of. But if your sister could run his records, maybe break into his banking so we can see who he's been working with, we might be able to figure out who wanted him dead and who might be next."

He looked away from me, pushed his fingertips to the bridge of his nose. "What about the other bodies?"

"Don't have IDs on them yet."

"We'll wait until we have their names. If we can't see an obvious connection...we'll go from there."

"We'll tap your sister's talents."

He pressed his lips together into a thin line. Body language said no. Connection between us said hell no.

But all he said was, "We'll find another way."

I scrubbed at my head and shrugged. "All right. Fine. Did you get anything on the Russian situation?"

Outside, beyond the closed door, Dash's laugh rolled out, mixed with Jolie's brazen chortle.

As soon as we'd gotten back from the morgue, the two of them had quickly fallen into a card game. It was a new game Dash had helped develop for the small company in Canada. The company that now wanted to hire him.

The game had opened the doors onto a wider audience for the company and it would open doors for Dash if he accepted their offer.

"Not much more," Terric said. "We have a contact number. She thinks if we call, they'll pick up."

"Why are we waiting on that?"

He crossed his arms over his chest. "I want to take this away from here. Leave Dash to look after her. Tonight."

"You're going to sneak out and talk to the Russian mob behind your sister's back?"

I could tell from the tug of guilt through our connection that that was exactly what he wanted to do.

"She's not the kind of person who wants to stand aside while someone else solves her problems," I said. "She's not a child, Terric."

"And how does her being there when we confront the mob make anything better?"

"I'm not arguing with you. I'm just warning you that she's going to kick your ass when she finds out you did this without her."

"We'll tell her," he said.

"Before we do it."

He paused, and I could feel the catch of his worry. "Fine," he said. "Before we do it."

"Good man. Now get out of my room. I want some shuteye."

He moved away from the door, opened it.

"Also, don't let Dash go," I said before he was out of the room. "Idiot loves you. Thought you should know that if he hasn't told you."

"I know."

"Then do me a favor and tell him you love him back."

"Worried about us? Careful, Shame. I might think you like having us around."

"I don't like having you around. Move out. Together. Go to Canada. Go to Mars. Just where ever you go, go together. I'm done with your angst."

"Oh, I don't think I have the market share of angst in this house."

"Blow me, Conley." I flopped back and pulled a pillow over my head.

Terric may have said something, but if he did, I didn't hear it.

Even though he shut the door behind him, I could feel the confusion of emotions he wrestled. Love and worry about Dash. Love and worry for Jolie.

Jesus. Man was all love and worry.

And yeah, a part of me wanted to just slip out and fix this Russian problem, and the Canada job problem without Terric.

I wasn't Jolie's brother or Dash's lover. They could be mad at me all they wanted and it wouldn't chew me up like it was chewing up Terric.

When had I started caring about things like that? Caring about Terric's hurt feelings?

Probably when the connection between us had turned into a two-way street.

Lucky me.

The phone in my pocket buzzed. I dug it out and put it to my ear, still under the pillow.

"What?"

"Manners, Shamus. Manners," Jak chided.

I shoved the pillow off my face. "Hey, Jak. I never gave you this number."

"I know how to find what I need."

She did. And I loved that about her.

"Thought you had a card game tonight," I said. "Did you come up short and need me to bail you out?"

"I don't come up short in anything I do. And if I did, I wouldn't call on a scrawny devil like you."

I made a small hurt sound. "Scrawny?"

"Boy, you should eat a sandwich once in a while."

"I'll put it on the calendar. Did you find what I need?"

She hesitated. When she spoke, her voice was a careful construction of cheer. "Come on by tonight. I'll be at the shop. I'll tell you there."

Pretty sure she was lying. Or distressed.

"Everything okay?" I asked.

"Everything will be. Just come by. I'll tell you what I know, and then we'll be done with all this, right?"

All this?

"Sure," I said. "Right."

I glanced at the bedside clock. It was six thirty and wouldn't be dark for a couple hours yet. "You there now?"

"I will be by the time you are."

"Good."

I pocketed the phone, pushed up on my feet and grabbed the hoodie off the floor where I'd tossed it. It had a couple holes in it and the sleeve was soaked with blood.

I lobbed it in the general direction of the bathroom hamper. Strode into the hall. Terric, Dash, and Jolie were in the living room, talking.

Good.

I ducked into Terric and Dash's room.

A little smaller than my room, it was still a large space. Unlike my room, which looked like I'd bought it pre-furnished and hadn't bothered with it since, their room actually reflected the two of them.

The room was clean, of course. I was surprised to see they'd painted the walls a soft cream. I didn't remember them painting it. Terric's art and some of Dash's pieces covered those walls in neat black frames.

Bed was new, another addition I hadn't noticed,

and covered in a deep blue, cream, and burgundy quilt. A small mountain of mismatched pillows crowded the carved wood and leather headboard.

Plants hung by the window, more on a small marble table by the bathroom door, and a couple others on the dressers.

I shook my head. When the hell had Terric crashing here because "I owed him" turned into Dash and him making it their home?

Apparently, sometime in the last year or so that they'd been living here.

Imagine that.

I found what I was looking for—Terric's pea coat hanging on a coat rack in the corner behind the door.

Checked the pockets for money—unfortunately, nothing—then shrugged into it.

Strolled through the living room where Dash and Jolie were playing cards over the coffee table. Terric perched on the arm of the couch next to Jolie, watching.

"Where?" he asked without looking up as I breezed past him.

"Out. Thanks for the coat."

"If you get blood on that—"

I slammed the door on the rest of his threat.

Night was coming on cold, but I felt the chill of something more than old winter storms in the air. I paused, one hand on the car door handle, my head tipped, listening.

Nothing but traffic and the wind stirring fir needles high above my head.

Maybe it was just nerves since, hey, I had been shot today, but I felt the need to make sure there was no one around the house.

I reached out with Death magic, just the lightest touch to sweep the heartbeats around the place. Dash, Jolie, Terric—who was curious as to why I was checking on them. Neighbors up the road a bit, and down. All normal. All the usual safe, non-killing people who should be here.

Good.

It took no time to get to Jak's place.

The shop looked closed except for a dull yellow light coming through the stained-glass windows. I walked up to the main door, tried it.

Open. Walked in.

"Jak?" I called. I didn't walk any farther down the blind aisles because I am not that stupid.

"Up here, Shamus. Why are you skulking around? Come in."

I let the door close behind me, glanced through the thin window out to the street. Nothing there. No one there.

Nothing my eyes could see.

Still, I was twitchy as hell.

"You gonna make me wait all night?" she asked. "I have a baby shower to get to in fifteen minutes."

I tucked hands in coat pockets and wove through the clutter up to the register where Jak sat. She'd traded her sequined shirt for one made of nothing but layers of pink feathers that fluffed with every breath she took.

"Stop staring at my bosom."

"Yes, Ma'am." I drew my eyes up to hers. "So. What did you find?"

"Those two dead men? Didn't have any enemies... well, not the kill-and-leave-you-in-an- alley sort of enemies. One had an ex-wife, but she went off and happily remarried twenty years ago."

"Did you get names on them?"

"Younger thinner man is Mike Durnam. He was a dentist with two offices. Other one is Doctor Raymond Tandy."

"Both medical guys?"

"Doctor of psychology."

"So, a dentist and a psychologist. Who had the ex-wife?"

"Psychologist."

"And when you say they didn't have any enemies?"

"Honey, a squeegee couldn't scrape dirt off them. Checked through their social circles. Don't see anyone they have in common." She slid a small piece of paper with their names across the counter to me.

I picked it up, stuffed it in my jeans pocket.

"Thanks. This will help." I tapped my knuckles on the countertop, thinking. Took a breath. Didn't smell oranges, though I'm not sure why I thought that was important.

"You didn't look any deeper into their affairs, did you?"

"You didn't pay me to. As a matter of fact, you didn't pay me to look this deep." She raised one eyebrow expectantly.

"Money." I grinned. "I was wondering when you'd ask me for it."

"I don't need money," she said. "I want your word."

"On?"

"You won't mix up Claire or her family in any of this."

I studied her. Tense at the corners of her eyes and mouth, fingers clenched in a fist. She looked worried. As well she should. If she had feelers out in enough places, she had a very good idea of exactly the things I'd been through, the things I had done in the past. She had a feel for just how dangerous those things were.

Jak had seen some bad years. I didn't doubt her when she'd told me she was retired. I hoped I hadn't pulled her back into something I'd need to get her out of.

"I promise you I will not let Claire, her family, or you be affected by any part of this. No one knows I came here. No one has to know. You have my word."

She watched me for a moment, her gaze flicking across my face. "Honey, someone always knows something. I do trust you, Shamus. And I am trusting you in this."

"Good choice. Do me a favor—forget I ever came here."

She chuckled with some relief. "I forgot about this the moment you walked in my door. Don't get me wrong. I'm glad to see you. But I'd rather you don't come asking me these kinds of questions again."

"Understood."

"Then you take care of yourself. Don't let those houseboys of yours tame you too much."

Houseboys?

I laughed and headed to the door. "It would be amusing to watch them try."

I pushed out into the falling dusk. Made it halfway to the car before the chill down my spine turned into a spike in my gut.

Someone was watching me.

Now.

Steady finger on a trigger. More than one finger. More than one heartbeat, slow. Even. Six. Six people.

Holy shit. Had Jak set me up for an ambush?

I stopped beside my car, hands down, fingers pointed at the pavement, beneath which still flowed the magic I wanted. Magic I could reach, I could use. Magic that was more than just a weapon in my hand.

Magic that flowed in my blood.

Six men. On the street. Moving my way. Shadows between buildings. Nothing more than quick glimpses out of the corners of my eyes.

Could be any half-dozen men who wanted me dead. I'd made plenty of enemies.

Could be the Russians. Although why they'd catch up with me here instead of my house didn't make sense.

"I'm giving you this chance to turn away now," I said loud enough the shadows would hear me. "One chance, mates."

I felt five of them pause. From the rhythm of the heartbeat, one did not. So he'd be the leader.

I waited.

Magic was fast, but bullets were faster.

It would take a lot of bullets to kill me. Even if they had that many bullets and intended to use them, I thought Death magic might just drag me back from the brink and force me to live whether my body liked it or not.

So, I had that hell scenario going for me.

"We just want information, Mr. Flynn." Leader stepped out from the shadows of the corner building in front of me, right hand free, left hand in the pocket of his coat.

Gun? Maybe.

White guy. My age or younger. Medium build. Slight Texan accent. I guessed not Russian.

"Information doesn't require firearms," I said.

"Perhaps you do," he answered.

He made no move. Just waited. All heartbeats in the area remained calm.

They weren't worried about me. Not enough to get their pulse rates up.

Good. That meant they didn't know me very well.

I put my hands out to both sides and slowly walked toward the guy. "I can be a very reasonable man. I actually prefer talk over taking a bullet. I'm all for agreeing that's what we're going to do here."

I wanted to get closer to him. Magic worked best when I put my hands on people. Back before it had been broken, you could throw a spell across half a city. But locking it away had changed the rules for how Terric and I could use it too.

We needed physical contact to do our worst.

That hadn't been much of a problem for me when I was killing one-on-one. But six against one weren't odds I liked.

"What's your name, mate?" I asked.

"Stop right there, or they'll shoot."

I stopped. About twenty feet away from him. I could feel four guys staked out on either side of the street parallel to me, the sixth behind me on the left. Heartbeats drumming. Steady, steady.

"All right," I said. "I'm standing here talking. Talk."

"How can we break into magic?"

"Excuse me?"

"The wall you and Mr. Conley erected around magic must come down. We want to know how to break that wall."

"Listen, pal. I don't know what you're talking about."

"But you do. A year ago, you and Mr. Conley fought a covert government program that would have weaponized magic. You closed magic behind a door no one can find and no one can open. If you tell us how to find that door...how to unlock that door...you will come to no harm."

"Like Lyle Carpenter came to no harm? And Mike Durnam and Raymond Tandy came to no harm? That kind of no harm?"

His heartbeat kicked up fast. Faster. So did the pulse of the five thugs around us.

They hadn't expected me to know that. Interesting.

"That was your handiwork, wasn't it?" I took a couple steps forward. "Did you ask them how to unlock magic too? Did they tell you just enough to get themselves killed for it?"

That was the million-dollar question that didn't add up. This joker wanted to know how to access magic. But whoever had killed those men had killed them with magic.

Someone knew how to get at it. Someone *was* getting at it.

And if it wasn't these assholes, then that meant there were some other assholes out there I had to track down.

"We are searching for magic, Mr. Flynn. Any trail. No one will stand in our way of finding it."

"Magic's gone."

He smiled. It was a heartless thing.

"We both know that's not true. There's enough magic in this world to injure. Enough to kill. You just said so yourself."

"Littering the city with corpses will get you noticed and dead," I said. "Why be that sloppy? A bullet would have blended in with every other murder. Why be so obvious with the magic kills?"

"We are looking for the person responsible for locking magic away. And here you are, Shamus Flynn, easy as that."

He drew his left hand out of his pocket. That was not a gun in his hand.

I had no idea what it was. It looked like a wooden stick. A pointer? A wand?

Seriously? A *wand*?

There are no wizards in this world.

Time did a weird thing.

No. Magic did a weird thing with time.

Split seconds slowed, crawled.

Death magic roared inside of me, rage filling my bones and flesh with the glorious bladed heat of magic looking for something, anything to devour.

The wizard pointed the stick at me and chanted.

Fuck the what?

Magic doesn't follow chants. Magic only shows up for duty if the magic user draws a glyph for it to fill. And then magic only enacts the nature of that glyph.

No chanting, no fucking wizards or wavy-wanding necessary.

But that man, and that wand, were channeling magic. A dark, sickening magic I'd never felt before. I didn't know how he was tapping it. Hell, I didn't even know where he was drawing it from.

I so didn't care.

I threw myself at him, punched his face.

The air filled with bullets and the stench of burnt oranges.

I came down hard on top of the guy.

He swung at me with the wand in his fist. Kicked to get free.

I caught his wrist, broke it. He yelled.

The wand fell onto his chest, then the sidewalk. I hauled him up into a choke hold, between me and the gunmen. Didn't track where the wand went.

They had said they were looking for magic, but they obviously already had it. Or maybe they only had some of it and they wanted more.

"Throw the guns out here. All of them," I said, holding the guy as my shield. "Do it and I'll let him go. Keep even one bullet on your body—I'll kill him. Then I'll kill each and every one of you."

Silence.

Death magic rolled in me, lashed out at the guy.

He yelled.

"I am not fucking around," I growled into his ear. "Call off your dogs. Now."

He lifted his hand to signal the men.

They stepped out of the shadows of the buildings. Five in total. Guns in one hand, wands in the other.

Bloody hell.

They chanted. Raised wands. Raised guns.

And fired.

The guy in my arms screamed through the first five or six shots that hit him. Then he stopped breathing and went silent, heavy, dead.

The gunmen unloaded their clips as I dragged the dead guy with me back toward a notch in the alley for cover.

Didn't make it.

Bullets hit my shoulder, broke my collarbone, shattered ribs in my chest.

Slick, hot blood sprayed over my face, stomach.

My arms went numb. Then legs. I stumbled.

Death magic, somewhere at a far distance, caught fire.

The world rock-a-byed sideways, taking me down.

Then pain kicked the hell out of whatever was left of me and everything went black.

CHAPTER 9

Light.

Pain.

Screaming.

I was under dark water. Drowning.

Hands broke through. Grabbed me. Dragged me up.

Into the light.

Into the pain.

I yelled.

"...got you. Easy. Easy."

Terric's voice.

Terric's hands on my face. On my chest.

I blinked away blood and blackout.

Terric leaning above me, eyes filled with fury and magic.

I tried to talk. He shook his head. "You're okay.

You're going to be okay now."

His voice was far away and garbled. I thought I felt the world humming beneath us. Were we moving? Were we in a car? Then everything slipped away again.

———

Someone had tucked me into a soft blanket. Soft bed, too. Pillow under my head. I was warm. I didn't hurt. I didn't feel much of anything, really.

All I wanted was to slip back into sleep before anything changed, but I heard someone inhale, then the crack of a chair adjusting as that person moved.

"Easy, Shame," Terric said, near me. His voice was clear. Tired, but there was none of that nightmare-garbled distance to it. "Don't try to move."

Which only made me want to move.

I settled for opening my eyes.

For a couple heartbeats, I thought I couldn't see. Then the low light gave fuzzy edges some clarity.

I was in my room. Terric sat in a chair next to the head of the bed, to my right. The door was behind him, but I thought it might be shut.

I had no concept of what time it was, what day it was. I was having a little trouble remembering what month it was.

"You were shot," Terric said. "Multiple times. I got

the bullets out. Healed you. But you're not in good shape right now, Shame. You still need to rest."

"How...?" My voice wasn't even a whisper. My mouth was ash dry, and it hurt just to breathe hard enough to make air into words.

He reached over and placed his hand on my chest. Cool, soothing magic flowed into me with a comforting weight.

He drew his hand away. I might have closed my eyes for a while.

"Can you drink?" he asked, maybe a moment, maybe an hour later.

I opened my eyes, expecting a beer. Got a straw sticking out of a glass of water.

"For fuck's sake," I said. More than a whisper this time, though my throat felt like I'd been gargling hot gravel.

He angled the straw to my mouth so I didn't have to lift my head much. I sucked down a couple gulps. After the third, it felt like my throat and mouth were working together again.

"How long have I been in bed?"

"Two days."

"Fuck."

He leaned back, put the glass down and rubbed at his eyes. "We found you...." He stopped moving, his fingers pinching at the inside corners of his eyes so that the width of his hands covered his face.

He cleared his throat. Started again.

"I felt the shots. Maybe not all of them, but the bad ones. The ones that killed you."

He dropped his hands into his lap and stared at me. His eyes were ice blue, ringed with red. And so very, very tired.

"Killed," I repeated.

"Killed," he agreed.

We both let that settle between us.

"I knew where you were, could feel you bleeding out..." His voice gave up, and I watched him stare blindly into that memory. A tear tracked unnoticed down the corner of his cheek.

"Dash drove," he went on. "I was blind with your pain. With the need for you not to die."

"You...healed me," I said.

"I brought you back from death." His eyes ticked down, gaze steady with a pain that did not reach his blank, emotionless face. "I let...magic do anything it wanted to bring you back. I didn't heal you. You weren't alive."

"Fuck," I said softly.

He nodded slowly.

I took a moment to evaluate my body. Breathing,

heart pumping. Sore and aching, but not in terrible amounts of pain.

Zero hunger for brains, so I guess that ruled out the zombie theory.

I was like someone who had drowned, or been frozen, or otherwise flat-lined and then had been brought back by forcible actions.

"What about the gunmen?"

He shook his head. "Just you lying there."

"And another dead guy."

He frowned.

"There should have been another dead guy with me. Shot up."

Shook his head again. "I didn't see anyone. I didn't see...anything but you. We had to go. Had to load you in the car fast. The police were on their way."

"They weren't the Russians," I said, trying and failing to pull myself into a sitting position. All I managed was to prop myself up better on my pillow.

"Don't," he said quietly.

For once, I listened to him.

"They wanted to know how to break into magic."

He stared at me for long enough, I wondered if he'd heard me.

"Terric?"

His eyes seemed to clear and focus on my face.

"Jesus. When did you sleep last?"

He shook his head.

"Where's Dash?"

"Here. I think." He looked over his shoulder as if expecting Dash to be standing behind him.

"Come here," I said.

He frowned at me.

"Sit here. Next to me. On the bed."

"I'm fine."

"You're a mess. Sit. Now. Don't make me get out of this bed and force you."

That got a thin smile out of him. He stood like everything in his body hurt, turned, sat on the edge of the bed.

"Now lie down."

"Why?"

"Because I said so."

To my surprise, he stretched out on the mattress beside me, on his side, his back toward me.

He exhaled a soft, exhausted groan.

"Get some sleep," I said. "We'll deal with this in the morning."

He was already snoring. And I was right behind him.

CHAPTER 10

The sound of a shower running and the smell of fresh coffee and bacon woke me.

Light filtered in through my window, bleeding around the pulled curtains. I stared at the ceiling and took stock of myself.

I felt...decent. Good. Like I'd gotten a nice hard sleep and needed food.

But first, the bathroom.

I shoved the blanket off, sat on the edge of the bed for a second. I was in my boxers and nothing else. Bright pink new skin scattered like pocked stars across my chest. I pressed my finger against one, felt the slight indentation of the skin and flesh there.

Bullet holes. Healed.

I inhaled, exhaled. Felt bones move with the stretch of my lungs.

Stiff, but no pain.

God damn, Terric was good.

I eased up to my feet and walked to the bathroom, pissed forever, then took a shower to wash off the sweat, old pain, and random blood stains.

Dragged on a pair of jeans and a T-shirt, walked barefoot out into the hall, then to the kitchen.

Heard voices in the kitchen. Dash, Jolie, and Terric.

Walked in.

"Hey," Dash said, startled to see me in the doorway. "Here, sit down, Shame."

He got up, pulled out his chair for me. Stood there like he wasn't sure if I might need a hand to make it the six steps to the chair.

"I'm good," I said. Had to clear my throat a little to push sound into the words. "Be better with coffee and bacon."

"Sure," Dash said, turning his chair out for me anyway.

"Hey, zombie," Jolie said. "Good to see you shambling."

"Thanks," I replied. "Pass the brains, will you?"

She smiled and pushed her plate of toast my way. She glanced over at Terric, then back at me.

I didn't know what he'd told her about me. About

us. About magic. About what he'd done to save me. But she was not stupid.

She must have seen them drag me in. Must have seen Terric in full Life magic mode, healing with his bare hands, pulling bullets out of my flesh.

Terric was at the stove, cooking pancakes. His back was toward us. A pile of pancakes about a foot high teetered on a plate next to him. There was at least half a dozen more on the griddle.

"Feeding an army today, Mother Teresa?"

He turned. Gave me a look.

I tipped my chin up. Dared him to tell me that what he'd done was wrong. That me being alive was some kind of mistake he regretted.

I owed him for my life. Every breath. If I got a chance—when I got a chance—I'd tell him so. I'd thank him.

He had a hard time accepting the mistakes he could make with the Life magic he carried. Worried about it even more than I worried about the mistakes I could make with Death magic.

How screwed up was that?

The connection between us was a snarl of emotions I couldn't sort. Relief, certainly, but a mix of other things: worry, anger, guilt, irritation, and yes, joy.

So basically: we were a mess.

"Did you miss me?" I asked. "Dash, did he pine for me while I lay sleeping?"

Dash chuckled.

"No," Terric said. "Nobody pined for you, Shame. I was just thinking of how much I'll miss the peace and quiet in the house now that you're not comatose. Pancake?"

"I'll take half that pile."

"Yeah, you will." He transferred six pancakes onto a plate and brought it to me.

"Thanks." I held the edge of the plate, but didn't support the weight so he had to hold it to keep it from falling.

He scowled at me.

"Thanks," I said again. For everything. For saving me.

I knew he felt that through our connection.

He nodded. "Eat your pancakes."

I took the weight of the plate so he could let go.

He turned back to the griddle, his shoulders no longer board-stiff with worry. The connection between us was filled with relief and mild irritation.

Normal.

Good.

Dash tipped his head toward Terric and mouthed *thank you* as he handed me coffee.

I could only imagine Terric had been a delight to live with the last few days.

I gave him a small toast with my mug, then took a sip, groaned. "God, that's good. What day is it?"

"Thursday," Dash took the seat next to me, carrying his own coffee.

I poured a gallon or two of maple syrup over the spongy stack of cakes. "How have things been while I vacationed in coma-land?"

"We've made some progress," Dash said.

"On what?" I shoveled pancakes into my mouth. An explosion of vanilla, sweet maple, and toasted nuts hit my mouth like a damn freight train that rumbled through my body. I held up a finger to Dash and closed my eyes while I chewed, moaning a bit.

Food never tasted so wonderful as after one has died.

Trust me on this.

Also, food cooked by a man who couldn't help but put Life magic, healing, thriving into it—especially when he was worried—was more than a little mouth-gasmic.

Everything in my body tightened for it, hungered for it, devoured it.

"You done making love to your food?" Terric asked as he sat at the table on my left.

I flipped him off, heard Jolie chuckle, and slowly

finished chewing. Only then did I open my eyes and wash it all down with hot, black coffee.

I almost felt human.

Terric slouched a bit in his chair, his long fingers wrapped around his cup. His eyes were clear—no red, no exhausted dark circles—no magic. Just blue.

One of the dangers of carrying magic in your bones is that magic will change you. Eat away at the boundaries of what makes you *you* until you aren't you anymore. You become a tool for magic, an extension of magic.

Terric, I was happy to see, was just Terric.

And that was good too.

"You were saying?" I asked Dash.

"We've made some headway on those names you got."

"Names?"

"Written on a slip of paper in your pocket," Terric said.

Right. Durnam and Tandy. The men Jak had ID'ed.

"We?" I asked, glancing at Jolie.

She raised her eyebrow. "I'm all up on your secret magic stuff now. Did the spit handshake and everything."

"Huh." I looked over at Terric. "I didn't think this relationship was on a spit-to-spit basis yet."

Terric shrugged one shoulder. She might be up on some of our secret magic stuff, but not all of it.

"What did *we* find on them?" I asked.

"They weren't a part of the Authority," Dash said. "Not directly. But there are a few people they had in common who were."

I continued making my way through the pancakes. Glanced up for him to go on.

Jolie spoke: "They were all professionals and, as far as we can tell, were respected by people who were a part of the Authority."

"So, they knew how to keep their mouths shut. Were they connected to the Authority before or after it went public?"

"Before," Dash said. "They didn't throw dirt once it did come out, didn't have any complaints about the people in the organization."

"Were most of their clientele Authority members?"

"No," Jolie said. "They had thriving practices. Hundreds of clients. Which is why it took us so long to narrow down why they would have been hit."

"And what did you narrow it down to?"

"Us," Terric said. "They're looking for us."

I put my fork down. The pancakes were demolished and I couldn't eat another bite. I swigged coffee and glanced over at him. "Who is looking for us? Why?"

"You said there should have been a dead guy on the street with you," he said. "Who? Why?"

I took a breath, hesitating, since I wasn't sure how much he wanted Jolie to know. Decided to take the direct route.

"They weren't the Russians. But they had guns. And wands."

Silence filled the room.

Terric stared at me, and I held that gaze. I knew he knew I wasn't lying.

The corners of his eyes tightened as he picked up on the memory of the experience from me. The raw, sick feeling of the magic the wand had drawn upon, the blast of magic that had accompanied every damn bullet that had killed the guy I'd used as a shield, and then me.

"You two want to let us in on that?" Dash asked.

"No price to pay?" Terric asked.

"Not that I saw."

"That's not how it works," he said.

"I know. But that's how it worked for them."

"How what worked?" Dash asked.

Terric looked away from me. "They used the wands to access magic. To direct it. To use it as a killing force."

"How do you know?" Jolie asked. She was glancing between the two of us. Curiosity was glossed over with a little panic. We'd spooked her. I had to guess she didn't know about our connection.

"They do that sometimes," Dash covered smoothly. "It's weird, right?"

She nodded. "I think you two have been around each other too long."

"See, Terric?" I said. "Even your little sister thinks you should move out."

"How many?" Terric asked.

"Men? Six total. They shot through the guy who I thought was their leader, trying to kill me."

"Holy shit," Jolie breathed. She looked a little shaken.

Sometimes I forgot what that kind of thing must sound like for people who didn't have to accept that they were a target every single waking moment of their life.

"I don't suppose they gave you any indication of who they are working for?" Terric asked.

"Accents say it's not the Russians. So, I don't think it's part of the mess you're in, Jolie."

She nodded and took a sip of tea, refusing to make eye contact with me.

"Which means they must be a part of the dead bodies we've found around town," I said. "They admitted as much."

"Anything else?"

"They know magic is gone, and they're looking for it. Thought I had some intel on that."

"They were using magic, though, right?" Jolie asked. "Why are they looking for it if they already have it?"

"Either they have a limited access to it," I said, "or they have a limited supply of it. All I know is they want more. A lot more."

Terric nodded, thinking it through.

"Who did Durnam and Tandy and Carpenter have in common?" I asked.

Dash was watching Terric and chewing on the inside of his cheek. Like he had something to say, but didn't want to say it to him. Here. Now.

Maybe because it was something that Jolie shouldn't know. Maybe because he and Terric still hadn't settled the moving-out-of-country doesn't equal moving-out-of-love thing.

"There's a man named Harold Thorne," Jolie said. "Have you heard of him?"

I frowned. "No."

"He was a client of all three of those men. They were his dentist, real estate agent, and psychologist when he was going through a divorce."

"At the same time?"

She nodded. "A few years ago. We think...well,

Dash and I think, maybe someone's trying to threaten him. Or force him out of hiding."

"He's hiding?"

Dash stopped staring at Terric. "No one's heard from him since the Authority went public."

"So, he's dead," I said.

"No record of his death," Dash said. "His bank account is still open. Credit cards active. It's just, as far as we can tell, no one has actually seen him for a couple years."

"Recluse?"

Jolie shrugged. "Even a recluse shows up on a street camera, goes to doctor appointments."

"Did he? Go to doctor appointments?"

"Records indicate he did. Credit records."

"He's got an address?"

"That's the weird thing." Jolie rose to retrieve her laptop from the living room. "He sold his house three years ago. Moved to a small—and I mean small—place on the outside of town. Surrounded by trees and some acreage. There's a driveway to it, but it's not even on the satellite maps."

"What does this guy do for a living?" I asked.

"Lawyer," Terric said.

"Did he make enough money to remove himself from the maps, or make enough enemies he had to?"

"We can assume one or the other," Dash said.

"So we go check out his place," I said. "See if our wizards are gathering up there."

"Walk into the home of your enemies?" Jolie asked. "That's stupid. Why not call the cops on them?"

"Cops can't handle this," I said.

She raised her eyebrows. "Weren't you just lecturing me about how I should have gone to the authorities—the police—with my problems?" she asked Terric.

"Yes," he said. "That's still true. You should have. The Russian mob isn't trying to kill people with magic."

"Dead is dead," she said. "They have guns. They're obviously not afraid to kill people—with guns or any other way. Walking in there is suicide."

Terric and I didn't say anything. I didn't know what expression we wore, but it must have been the same. She looked between the two of us and shook her head.

"That's...freaky."

"Speaking of the Russians," Dash said, changing the subject. "We set up a meeting with them for tonight."

"We did what now?" I asked.

"Fuck," Terric exhaled. "You contacted them? Without telling me?"

"Shame was sleeping," Jolie said, "and you

were...well, you weren't sleeping or doing anything else. We got a hit on a direct line to contact someone up the food chain and we did some work feeling it out."

"And?" I asked. "Who are we meeting, where, when?"

Dash got up, brought the coffeepot over and refilled our cups. "His name's Art..."

"Doesn't sound Russian," I said.

He threw me a *shut-up* look. "As far as we can tell, he's a couple levels above the guy Jolie was working for. He assures us he can bring this to a resolution to make this problem go away."

"Good thing that doesn't sound like a threat," I muttered.

"When?" Terric asked.

"Seven tonight," Dash said. "Down at the waterfront."

"Plenty of space," I said.

"Plenty of witnesses in case something goes sideways," Jolie said.

"Who do they want to see?" I asked.

Jolie shrugged. "Me."

"No," Terric and I said at the same time.

"I don't think they care about what you want, Terric," she said. "If they see you—any of you," she pointed at each of us, "they're just going to walk away and kill me quietly. I'll meet with him. See what kind of deal I can make."

"You aren't going alone," I said.

"God, I hope not." She grimaced. "I don't want to be some Russian's target practice. I'm counting on all of you to be there, right beside me. Well, hidden. With guns. Beside me in spirit."

I glanced over at Terric. Waited to see if he was going to give up on that scowl. Even I could tell there was no talking her out of it.

"She's going to have to deal with this mess she got into," I said. "She can do it. We'll be there to make sure nothing happens to her."

He inhaled, sipped his coffee. "You will wait for us to come home. You swear you won't go without us."

"Swear," she said.

"Where are you going?" Dash asked.

"To see what Harold Thorne has to say about the dead bodies in town," Terric said.

"You and Shame?" Dash asked.

"About time." I stood, stretched. Was grateful when nothing snapped.

"I'll drive," Dash said.

"Nope," I said. "Not invited."

"You were half dead just a few hours ago. Terric does not make good decisions when that happens. If it happens again—"

"—it won't. It's not like I get shot every day."

"The last two times you went out of this house you got shot," Dash said.

"Coincidence."

"I'm driving," he said again.

"Terric," I whined. "Make him listen to me."

"He's driving." Terric stood. "Get your shoes, Shame. Jolie, promise you'll stay here."

"With all the doors locked," she said. "You'll be back before seven?"

"Yes. This should only take a couple of hours. Be careful. Be safe. If anything goes wrong, call the cops." He bent, gave her a quick kiss on the top of her head.

Then he and Dash walked out of the room.

"Shame?" Jolie asked before I'd taken more than two steps toward my room. "You didn't see him. These last couple of days."

"Who?" I walked down the hall and she followed me.

"Terric." She leaned in the doorway to my room, both hands in her back pockets.

I pulled on socks, boots.

"I don't know what kind of *thing* you have between you," she said. "Dash told me you're not lovers."

She waited, one eyebrow up.

"Dash is one hundred percent correct on that."

I grabbed a T-shirt out of my drawer. Sniffed it to see how clean it was. Clean enough.

"It's just that, well, there's three of you living here. I've seen how Terric and you look at each other. And I can tell Dash and Terric are fighting about something."

I tried not to laugh. "They are not fighting about Terric and me being in love. I'm straight. Very," I made a line with my hand, "straight. He's in love with Dash." I laced my boots.

"They're fighting over a job thing that might require one or, dear God, please," I rolled my eyes to the heavens and pressed my palms together, "both of them moving out."

"Okay," she said, "fine. But he...he really cares for you. He blamed himself for you going out there like an idiot and getting shot like an idiot."

"Strange. Usually, he just blames me for being an idiot." I gave her a smile.

She did not return it. "If he gets hurt, if you do some stupid thing to get him hurt, I'm blaming you for anything that happens to him. Do you understand me? Keep yourself safe, keep my brother safe."

"One of those things is usually my goal."

"Make him absolutely your goal. You don't want to know what I'll do to someone who hurts my brother." She cracked her knuckles just in case I didn't get her message.

I got the message.

"You know Terric can take care of himself." I shrugged into the T-shirt.

"So?"

"It's just, out of the two of us, he's the one who usually comes out of these things unbloodied."

"He's missing a finger because of something you two got mixed up in a couple of years ago."

Right. I tended to forget about the finger since he didn't make a big deal about it.

Also, I felt guilty as hell about it.

Not that I could have saved him at the time he was losing the finger, since I happened to have been dead then.

"Did he tell you about that?"

"Dash did."

Mental note: tell Dash to keep his mouth shut.

"He tell you anything else about that something we got mixed up in?"

"Only that you both almost died. And that it had something to do with magic. He wouldn't tell me what."

We hadn't almost died. We had actually died. Terric had been tortured by an asshole named Eli Collins who wanted to weaponize magic—that's how he lost his finger. We'd killed Eli. Messily.

And we'd shut down the organization that had

turned living breathing people into walking magical bombs.

That was why magic was locked away. It wasn't just because Terric and I are Soul Complements—two magic users perfectly matched who can make magic do things it was never intended to do.

We'd chosen to put magic in a timeout to keep it out of the wrong hands.

Mankind had proven just how asinine it could be with that kind of power readily available. We thought maybe a few decades away from that temptation would do the world, and all the people in it, some good.

"Are you going to tell me?" she asked.

"Nope. It's old shit that no longer applies to the rules of this world."

"This world has rules?"

"Magic does."

"Yeah. Strange how that all changed around the same time you two got out of that mess you got into and then decided to move in together."

"Our living arrangements have nothing to do with the laws of magic," I lied.

"Sure," she said.

"Shame!" Dash called. "You coming?"

"Get off my back, Mom!" I yelled.

I gave Jolie a wink. "Lock the doors behind us. Don't let anyone in."

I started down the hall.

"More rules?"

I opened the door. Looked back at her. "I'm serious."

"Do you get that many visitors?"

"Only the occasional family member running from the Russian mob. If a sibling shows up, I'd suggest slamming the door in his or her face before they make your life a complicated mess."

"Ha-ha." She took the door out of my hand.

"Lock it."

"I will."

And just because she was Terric's little sister, and we were leaving her alone for the first time since she had hit town, I waited on the other side of the door until I heard the locks turn and the chain slide into place.

CHAPTER 11

We took Terric's car. Dash drove. Terric sat in the front seat and I lounged in the back.

"You two figure out the job in Canada yet?" I asked.

"We're not dealing with that in front of you, Shame," Terric said.

"Well, you're not really dealing with it anywhere else, either. How long before you both admit that you just want to stay here in Portland?"

"Job's in Canada," Terric said.

"Job's anywhere," I said. "They made this thing called the 'Internet'. Real handy. Dash can do the game designing online."

"Still not dealing with that now," Terric said.

"Seriously, Shame," Dash said. "We have enough disasters on our hands."

"Speaking of which," I said, "how much did you really tell Jolie?"

He shrugged. "I kept it general. But it's not like I can pretend nothing is happening when we're dragging your barely breathing body into the house and Terric has gone all blue-glow eyes and Faith healer hands."

"So, she knows he uses magic?"

"Yes," Terric said. "We told her both you and I have remnants of magic in our bodies. We told her it was because of all the shit we went through a year ago. And no, we didn't tell her exactly what that shit was. Just that we'd been a part of taking down some maniacs who had killed a lot of people on their rise to the top and who were doing very bad things with magic."

"She let it go at that?"

He sighed. "Not for long, I'm sure."

"And that's when you and she tracked down the Russians and our boy Harold Thorne?"

"She knows her shit," Dash said. "Got into records I would have had a hard time breaking."

"Don't get used to it," Terric said. "She's going back to Seattle after this."

"I know," Dash said. "And I think she should. Her family and friends are there. But if the Authority was still a going thing, I would have hired her in a flat second."

"Maybe you can take her with you to Canada," I suggested.

They both went silent again.

"Or not," I said.

"What else do you know about the men who killed you?" Terric asked, maybe to remind me that I was only alive because he had taken pains to see that I was. "They had wands?"

"Wands in one hand, guns in the other. Mix of ages, mix of races. All male, I think. They killed the hell out of the guy who I thought was their leader. I'm going to guess there is an opening for upward movement in their organization."

"You sure they're not the Russians?" Dash asked.

I absently rubbed at one of the bullet holes over my heart. "I don't know. The accents sounded American. But there's...I don't know. Something."

"What something?" Dash asked.

"They were coordinated. Determined. Like they were used to working together in that way. It wasn't the first time they'd drawn on magic with those wands."

"Some kind of splinter group in the Authority gone rogue?" Dash asked.

"Or a group from outside the Authority," Terric said. "Government?"

I shook my head. "I don't think it's government. Didn't have that vibe. The leader said they weren't sloppy. That they were killing with magic and leaving the bodies behind to be found for a reason. You said you thought they wanted to find us. By us do you mean you and me?"

Terric nodded. "From what Dash and Jolie dug up, I'm assuming they're looking for how to bring magic back into the world and they think you and I are mixed up in it. They might even think we're the ones who locked it away."

"So, you *were* listening to us," Dash said. "I thought you were catatonic the last couple nights."

"No, I heard you. And Jolie. I just...I just couldn't answer. Life magic was...it took all of my attention to deal with it."

"You're right," I said. "They do think we locked it up. Which means either they are very good guessers or someone who knows what we did told them."

"The people who know what we did make for a pretty short list," Terric said.

I nodded. "Cody Miller. Allie and Zayvion. Davy and Sunny. Detective Stotts and Nola. Maybe Violet and Kevin, and my mum and Hayden."

"That's not exactly a short list," Dash said.

"Do you think any of those people would tell someone that we were the ones who locked magic away, Shame?" Terric asked.

I thought it over. All of those people had fought

and nearly died beside us. More than once. To keep the Authority secret. To keep magic safe and out of the hands of people who tried to do horrible things with it.

So, no. They would never tell anyone that we had locked it up. Not even under torture.

Well, maybe Cody Miller. He and I had run on the wrong side of the law, not to mention a couple mobs when we were too young to be out past curfew.

But Cody had made huge sacrifices to make sure magic was safe and locked away, too. For many years, he'd given up his sanity for it.

I knew he wouldn't go around talking about what we'd done.

"I don't think so," I said. "Cody, maybe. No one else. And I don't think he'd rat us out. He has as much reason to want magic safely out of reach as we do."

"Except you both can still reach magic," Dash said.

"Yeah, well, it's possible Cody can too. Not how he used to, but he acted as the focal point for us to fix magic. There's some chance he might have an 'in' on it."

"Have you talked to him lately?" Terric asked.

"Had a beer with him a couple weeks ago."

"And?"

"Same old Cody."

Terric nodded. "It can't be him. So we're looking at

some kind of rogue group of magic users who just happened to find a way to access magic with wands?"

"About that," Dash said, "I'm curious. Can either of you tell when someone is accessing magic?"

"I can when they're throwing it at my head," I said.

"No. I mean did you feel someone get into the magic? Break into it?"

"No," Terric and I said at the same time.

"Don't you think that's weird?"

"I think all of this is weird," I said.

Terric was silent. Because, yes. That was weird.

Not that Terric and I had locked magic away with warning bells attached. We were connected to magic, carried magic. If someone was getting into it, we should have felt something.

Shouldn't we?

"Or the magic they're using isn't connected to all magic?" I suggested. "It's stashed away? Maybe they've found a storage of magic?"

"Like the disks Allie's dad made to hold magic?" Dash asked. "Those were destroyed, weren't they?"

"Absolutely," I said. "So that can't be it."

"Or could it?" Terric asked. "Allie's father can't have been the only magic user in history who came up with the idea of portable magic. Maybe that's where the wands play into all this."

Dash glanced at me in the rearview mirror. "Were

the wands carrying the magic, or were they pulling magic out from behind the locks you and Terric put on magic?"

"I'm not sure. You didn't see anything on the street near me?"

"Blood and guts," Terric said.

"Beside that. The guy who died dropped his wand."

"No wands, no bodies," Dash said. "Nothing but you lying there. And if Terric hadn't had been with me, I'm not sure I would have seen you. You fell in the shadow of the alley."

"Really wish I'd been conscious when you found me."

"Really wish you'd been alive," Terric said quietly.

Yeah. I was still dealing with the horror of that too.

"This is it," Dash said, slowing the car.

We were on a two-lane highway west of town. We'd been traveling down it for a while, businesses giving way to houses, houses giving way to farms, farms giving way to hilly fields strung with grapevines, and finally, vineyards giving way to tree cover, the occasional glimpse of a creek, and not a lot of anything else.

An opening between the trees to our right, and a rutted driveway leading deeper into those trees, was the only hint that man had ever wandered that way.

"No mailbox, no fence," Terric said. "I thought this

was a fortified place."

"It's off the grid," Dash said. "We don't know how fortified it might be. But I wouldn't rule it out. I'll get the guns out of the trunk."

My stomach clenched. For all that I had been killed more than once in my life, for all that my death had far too often come from me being on the wrong side of a weapon's discharge, it sure didn't make being on the right side of a firearm any easier.

As a matter of fact, I was beginning to build up a nice little phobia around guns.

Dash killed the engine and got out of the car. Terric remained in the passenger's seat.

"Are you going to be okay on this?" he asked.

I could try to bullshit him and tell him I was fine. Wouldn't work.

He could feel the cold sweat of fear I was trying to ignore just as clearly as I could feel his calm concern.

"Getting tired of being shot," I said.

"You don't have to go in there with us," he said. "I'd actually rather you didn't."

I pulled a cigarette out of my pocket and tapped it on the back of my hand. "I know. But I can't let you go in there without me, either. You want me to try to talk Dash into staying behind?"

He shook his head. "We'll keep him safe. I don't think he's in a stay-behind mood lately anyway."

"Terric. Talk to him. Make it right for both of you."

He inhaled, his mouth pressing in a frown. "Let it go, Shame."

"I just think—"

"Please."

And the emotions behind that, the mix of love and guilt and hope and pain, were enough to shut me up.

"All right," I said. "All right. Let's go talk to the lawyer."

I opened the back door, stood into the brace of wind. It was cool today, cloudy, the road and trees shadowed.

I walked around to the back of the car. The trunk was open.

The memory of the woman I'd loved all too briefly, Dessa Leeds, appeared out of nowhere and stopped me flat. She'd drugged me and thrown me in a trunk a lot like this one, then tied me up and interrogated me in a cheap motel.

I couldn't help but smile.

It was the best first date ever.

Damn, I missed her.

Terric clapped his hand on my shoulder as he walked past me. At that contact, the memory of Dessa and the pain of her death was gently pushed back into all the other pains of my life that would never fade.

I took a breath and focused on the arsenal in the

trunk. Whistled.

"I had no idea we were gunning for bear," I said. "Or elephant?" I bent my head against the wind and lit my cigarette. Filled my newly healed lungs with tar and nicotine.

My head cleared instantly.

Nice.

Dash slipped an Uzi over his shoulder and tucked a Baretta in his belt.

Terric stood with his arms crossed over his chest, the epitome of calm, and stared at the contents of the trunk with a mixture of amusement and worry. "I see you got into Shame's no-no room in the basement."

"It's called an armory, thank you very much," I said.

Dash handed Terric a revolver. "I know neither of you can throw magic like the old days. It's all a hands-on kind of thing now. We might not have a chance to get that close."

See, here's the funny thing. Terric and I had closed magic away a year ago. Dash had been living with us for nearly that entire time. And we hadn't really sat down and told him how we could use magic.

Or at least I hadn't.

From the way Terric nodded, I realized I hadn't been invited to their heart-to-heart talks about magic.

Not that I expected Terric to keep Dash in the dark

about this stuff. If I had a lover, if I had anyone who cared for me as much as Dash cared for Terric, I'd tell them all my deep, dark secrets too.

Well, most of them.

Okay, some of them. Maybe.

Relationships needed a little mystery, right?

Terric took the gun, checked the chamber, accepted the extra ammo Dash offered.

"Shame?" Dash asked, waving a hand at what was left in the trunk.

The sight of all those guns made my stomach turn again. But I was not going to get into another shootout without at least some of the bullets coming from my side.

I chose a handgun, stuck it in my waistband, and took an extra clip.

"That it?" he asked.

"How many people do we think might be in there?" I asked.

Dash shrugged and shut the trunk. "Could be a dozen. Could be no one. We couldn't get any good leads on the comings and goings out here."

"Swell," I said. "Let's go introduce ourselves to Mr. Thorne and find out why all those men who knew him are dead."

I started down the dirt driveway between the trees, Terric to my right, and Dash on my left.

CHAPTER 12

The driveway curved back into the trees for about a quarter of a mile, and a narrow wooden bridge just wide enough to roll a car across spanned a creek that was fast and swift from early snow melt.

Right on the other side of that bridge sat the cabin. It really was a small place. Single story, cedar shake shingles on the walls and roof, two small windows on either side of a narrow, windowless door.

No smoke coming out of the stone chimney. No light coming through the windows. A small moss-covered garage was attached to the left of the building, door shut. From the growth of weeds and moss covering the driveway, vehicles hadn't been down this way for months.

We stood on one side of the bridge, tucked in an

overhang of trees that hadn't been trimmed in a year at least.

Dash pulled binoculars up to his eyes and scanned the house and the area around it.

"I don't see anyone. Or any signs of habitation," he said.

Terric glanced at me. I shrugged. Either one of us could use magic to sense if there were any hearts beating in the area. But if someone was out here who could use magic, would they feel Terric and me using it?

That's not the way magic used to work. I thought it was worth the risk.

I reached out with Death magic. Could feel the strong rhythms of Terric's and Dash's hearts, the faint tapping of birds and squirrels and other small creatures. Didn't feel any other breathing human in at least a mile radius.

"I think it's empty," I said.

Terric strode across the bridge, I followed, Dash behind me.

I could tell Terric was using Life magic to check out the cabin too. The weeds in the driveway bent as if a wind had just brushed a palm over them, even though the air was still.

"Traps?" Dash asked quietly.

"Don't think so," I said. "Terric?"

"It's been at least a month since someone's been out here."

"Did they leave any protection behind?" Dash asked.

Terric paused, his hand halfway to the door handle. Tipped his head down. This time I could feel the light wash of magic he pushed out into the space around us.

And yes, it felt good.

"I don't think so." He tried the handle. It was locked.

"Here," I said. "Let me get that."

I reached over for the doorknob and let the Death magic in me destroy the wood holding it in place. I pulled the handle out through the door and dropped it to one side.

"Subtle," Terric noted.

"Efficient," I said. "And easy. Two of my favorite words."

I shouldered the door open. It swung inward easily. Stepped in and flicked on the light switch.

"Rustic," I said.

The single room opened to a small double bed in an alcove ahead and to the left, and a small kitchen with a single basin sink, two burner stove, and mini-fridge to the right.

A tired couch sat the center of the room, a wooden

crate at its side balancing a desk lamp. The card table in the corner of the room stood half-buried under a pile of paper, books, file folders, and dust.

The largest piece of furniture in the room was a built-in bookcase which began at the wall to my left, continued across the next wall over the table, hopped up and framed the top of the doorway above the sleeping nook, and stretched across the walls to the right.

Basically, every spare inch of cabin wall was filled with books.

"So, this is where old librarians go to die," I said.

Terric strolled off to my right, muttering quietly.

"See a title you like?"

Dash frowned, then headed to the left. "Holy shit," he said quietly.

I glanced at him. "Really? If this impresses you, we need to take a field trip to a magical place called a 'bookstore'."

"They're more than books, Shame," Terric said. "They're magic books."

I walked across the room and browsed the pile of papers on the card table, then scanned the shelf behind it.

There was a lot of homework involved in being a part of the Authority. Years of reading and studying histories. Years of learning and perfecting glyphs, years of bearing the pain for calling on magic, and then making magic do exactly what one wanted it to do.

That was all on top of the physical training—defense, offense, attack—specific to the branch of magic one decided to specialize in.

I had read a warehouse full of books on magic—many of them volumes the common magic user had never seen.

"I don't recognize any of these titles," I said.

"Neither do I," Terric said. "Not one of them."

I had been a good student, but Terric had run academic magical circles around me. He was all Honors and Excellents and gold stars with pluses and cherries on top. For him to say he didn't recognize any of the titles, well, that meant something.

"None of them?" I tried to get my head around the statistical impossibility that Terric hadn't heard of, or laid eyes on, at least one of the titles.

"Not yet." He continued along the wall, nearly in the kitchen area now.

"Dash?" I asked.

Dash had a different history with magic. I hadn't known him back in the days when the Authority was a secret organization.

He said he did some bookwork for a few people who had been a part of the organization. But he'd really gotten to know about the darker aspects of magic when he'd come to work for Terric and me when we'd been tapped to deal with the fallout from the Authority's unsecreting.

That was, of course, after magic had been softened, gentled, tamed.

Then Eli and the government agency he worked for had decided to destroy that.

In those few years with us, Dash had proven to have a very long reach when it came to records and resources both well-known and obscure.

He was a damn genius at getting his hands on information. Within a year he had done a decade's worth of studying all things magical.

"Nothing looks familiar to me," he said.

"So, we have a bibliophile hoarder of rare magical books?"

Terric pulled a book off the shelf and thumbed through it. "Very rare. The kind of magic used in this volume isn't what they taught in the Authority."

"So, it's what?" I asked, "Potions? Voodoo?"

"Some of that, yes," he said. "This one?" He held it up. "Explains how to access magic in dead zones where it's unavailable. Also, how to store it in objects."

"Shit," I said. "Objects like wands?"

He shrugged. "Probably."

Dash stepped away from the shelf. "Why would a

lawyer stash all these books out here? It must have taken years to collect them."

"A lawyer should be smart enough to know a remote cabin with a non-existent security system is just asking for these things to be stolen," I said.

"And they're crumbling," Terric noted. "Some of these are very old. They should be stored in a museum, or at least in a controlled environment."

I glanced at the desk again. "Then we're thinking this was some kind of temporary solution?" I picked up a letter on top of the pile and flicked it to get the dust off. "This is dated two years ago."

Terric glanced around the room. "Think he was running?"

Dash moved into the bedroom area, opened drawers. "Nothing here. If he was running, he didn't stay."

I strolled to the kitchen, and Dash went over to dig through the papers on the table. I checked the cupboards. "There's a couple months' worth of food." I picked up a can of chili and read the packing date. "Two years old."

Terric pinched at the bridge of his nose. "So, he... what? Thought he needed a place off grid to hide and brought all these books out here, stocked the place, then never set foot in the cabin again?"

"Maybe," I said. I opened what I thought was a

pantry door. Saw stairs leading down. "I'll check the basement."

I tugged on the pull string light, glanced at the wooden stairs—dust and no footprints—then started down. The ceiling was low, open framework with electrical wires strung through the strips of insulation. The walls were made of concrete foundation blocks and the floor was dirt.

The man stripped half-naked and lying in the middle of the room, however, was dead.

Fuck.

"Shame?" Terric walked down the stairs. "Oh, shit."

"I'm assuming this is our lawyer," I said.

It was a little hard to tell since the body was decomposed to the point past both bloat and stink, but I was pretty sure magic was involved in the death.

For one thing, the dirt floor around him was carved with glyphs that ringed his prone body in a circle.

For another, glyphs were burned into his flesh across forehead and bare chest. A dark tattoo that might have once been a fish curved out from beneath the glyph burned into his chest.

"Do we know what he used to look like?" I asked.

"Hey, I think I found something." Dash came down the stairs. He stopped when he saw the body on the floor. "Jesus."

"Do you have a picture of Harold Thorne?" Terric asked.

Dash opened the file folder he was carrying and pulled out a photograph. "This is him," he said.

Alive Harold Thorne looked to be in his late sixties. He also looked like a guy who didn't smile much and spent too many years hitting the bottle. He was dressed in a white shirt and tie, all buttoned up so there was no chance to see the tattoo.

"About the same build," I said. "Could be him."

"Check his pockets," Terric said.

"What do I look like? Frisker of the dead?" I whined, even though I was already kneeling beside the corpse and making busy.

Terric was getting that dangerous look in his eyes. I could feel Life magic pushing at him, though the very idea of him resurrecting this guy was pure horror-movie fodder.

Dead guy wore dress slacks, a belt, and still had on dark socks and shoes. I searched his front pockets. Nothing. Checked to make sure I wasn't going to step in the middle of a glyph carved in the floor, then propped him up enough I could slide my fingers into his back pocket.

Tugged free his wallet.

Flipped it open and stood.

"Harold J. Thorne," I read from his driver's license.

"Shit," Dash said. "The one guy all the other dead guys are connected to. And he's inked with the fish."

"So how does this break down?" I asked. "Was there some kind of secret they shared? Something to kill them all for? This cabin? These books? That tattoo?"

"If it was the books, they wouldn't still be here," Terric said. "Same with the cabin."

He walked around me to stand on the other side of Mr. Thorne. "The glyphs burned into him aren't the same as the other glyphs on the other victims."

"Huh," I said. "Binding carved on the forehead though, right?"

Terric squatted down on his heels, hands propped on his knees, fingers pressed together. "Yes, though with the decomposition it's hard to make out. Chest is..." he tipped his head sideways. "Does that look like Proxy?"

I shook my head. "No Proxy glyph I've ever seen. Well, half of it might have been a crap attempt at Proxy. What's the other one? Surrender?"

"Maybe," Terric agreed. "But it's rough. Glyphs that far off shouldn't be able to hold magic for a split second. And this looks like..."

"Like a four-year-old carved it mid-temper tantrum?" Dash asked.

I nodded.

"Here's a theory," Dash said. "What if those aren't the glyphs we think they are?"

I waved a hand at the corpse. "They're glyphs, Dash."

"Yes. They are glyphs. But what if they're not sloppy? What if they're modified? Changed so they can actually pull magic out from where it's locked away? You changed the rules of magic. Maybe the rules of how it can be accessed and what kind of glyphs will hold it have changed too."

"Fuck," I said.

Magic was a lot like water—it got where it wanted to go no matter how convoluted the route to get there might turn out to be.

"What did you find?" Terric asked.

Dash handed him the file folder. "Pictures of the other dead men and Harold. Two other men and four women we haven't seen. And a printout of names and numbers."

"Phone numbers?" I asked.

Terric shook his head. "Three digits."

"Address maybe? Area code?"

"I don't think so." He fingered through the pages. "Looks like an inventory list maybe?" he said. "Or a cataloguing of something?"

Dash nodded. "There's a name on the back of the last page."

Terric turned to it. "Pisces," he said. "Zodiac sign of the fish?"

"Name of the organization, or group they belong to," Dash said. "There are other files up there. Lists of names, all under the heading of Pisces. Dating back at least two decades."

"Birthday and horoscope club?" I said.

"Part of the Authority?" Dash asked.

"It's possible." Terric stood. "There were always subgroups and politicking going on. It wouldn't surprise me that there were a few secret groups within the group."

"What does the fish have to do with it?" I asked. "And what the hell was their group a part of that led them to this kind of death?"

"It will take some time to sort through the papers up there," Dash said. "Maybe there's something in them that explains all this."

"So these...shitty glyphs hold magic?" I asked.

"One way to find out." Terric handed Dash the folder then pulled out a pocketknife. He crouched down next to the corpse, studied the marks, then sketched the Proxy glyph into the dirt floor.

"Wow," I said. "That is the worst glyphmanship I've ever seen out of you, Ter. D+ and the plus is only because you used a pocket knife like a big boy."

"Shut up, Shame." He stood and took a few steps backward. "Let's see what it does."

I could feel the tension tighten the connection between us. Decided to take a couple steps back myself.

Terric called on magic, reaching toward it, where it flowed beneath the earth, where he and I could still get at it, and sending it into the glyph.

That would have worked in the old days. Should have worked now if the dead body told us anything.

I waited. We all waited.

Nothing.

"That's a bust," I said. "Nice theory about the new rules, though, Dash."

"One attempt does not a theory disprove," Dash said. "Did they do anything with those wands except point them at you?"

"They chanted," I said.

"Could have mentioned that before," Terric said.

"I was dead before."

"Still not okay with you joking about that nightmare," Terric said. "Do you remember what they were chanting?"

I thought about it, tried to form the syllables in my head.

"It was nonsense. Something like: 'lictu, lambas, boreal, noctu'."

The glyph exploded into a ball of flame.

"Shit!" Dash grabbed for Terric.

"No!" I lunged for both of them.

Too late.

The fire—magic fire—arced to Terric like a flame to oxygen. He threw up his arms to shield his face. The magic burned a glyph into his flesh and filled the room with a nauseating mix of scorched meat and rotten oranges.

Then the fire was gone, magic was gone, and the basement was quiet and dark again.

Terric ticked his gaze toward me. Blood covered his face. His chest. "That wasn't so..."

His eyes rolled up into his head and he screamed.

"Get him down," I yelled as I helped Dash manhandle him to the floor where he writhed and yelled.

"Shame," Dash said. "Do something!"

"Get his shirt off."

I held him down while Dash broke the buttons off his shirt and dragged it up over his head.

I could feel the magic push through him like a sickness worming into his flesh, his muscles, his bones. Life magic burned bright against it, but even with the magic he carried, this magic, this twisted sickness that had just burned into him was eating through Terric's body.

As quickly as Life magic healed him, this dark magic destroyed him.

Excruciating pain poured through our connection. I was covered in sweat. Shaking. Swallowed whole by his agony.

I wanted to scream right along with him.

I set my jaw and got busy reciting swear words instead.

I was not going to fucking pass the fuck out.

"Shame," Dash yelled. "Don't you pass out on me."

"I'm good," I growled. "Don't let go of him."

I tapped the Death magic that filled me, hard. Precise.

Here's the tricky part: Death magic devours. The completely dead guy behind me wasn't much of a meal. But the man in terrible pain whom I knelt over? The man to whom death would be a mercy? Terric?

Well, Death magic wanted to devour his life and give him the grim, final mercy.

Except I was standing in its way.

Just because the best thing Death magic did was kill things didn't mean it was the only thing Death magic could do.

Death could be an easing, a lessening of suffering, of pain.

Death was an ending. But that didn't mean it had to destroy.

Death could be a pause.

Magic can be wielded very easily like an ax. Draw a glyph, fill it with magic—with fire, with pain, with impact—and you're gonna get the job done.

But magic is much, much more difficult to wield precisely, with finesse, with restraint.

My hands were shaking so hard, I had to inhale and blow air out several times just to get control of them.

"Try to keep him steady," I said, maybe loud enough for Dash to hear over Terric's moans of agony.

I drew Death magic into my hands, into my fingers. Then I bent over Terric and very carefully traced my fingertip over the glyph that was burning in his body.

I killed the magic, cooled the flame, eased the pain, and cauterized the wound across his arms and chest.

Pain between us lowered to a sickening ache. I slashed my finger across his right arm, left, then chest.

Death magic canceled the glyph, canceled the magic.

Terric went dead still.

"Terric?" Dash said, had been saying. "You're okay. You're going to be fine. We got you. We got you."

I placed my hand over Terric's heart. Felt the stroke of fast, even beats.

"What are you doing?" Dash asked. "Shame?" He

clamped fingers around my wrist and squeezed until I could feel the pain. "What are you doing?"

I glanced up at him.

I don't know what he saw in my eyes. If I had to guess, it would be rage and sorrow and death.

"Talk to me right now, or I swear I'll knock you on your ass," he said.

Had to give it to the guy. He never backed down. Not even when he was staring death in the eyes.

"I'm going to put him in a deep sleep. So he can heal."

"A coma?"

"No. Close, but no." I was calm. Sounded reasonable.

Odd, since everything inside me was raging to kill. "You go get the car, bring it as close to the house as you can."

"I'm not leaving him with you," he said.

The corner of my mouth twitched upward. "Good instincts. But what choice do we have?"

"You go get the car."

"The only reason he's not screaming is because I am bearing half of the pain he's in. Do you want me to lose focus on that? Let him bear this pain alone?"

He paused. Swallowed. Made his decision. "I'll get the car."

Bless him for trusting me.

"If you kill him, Shame, I will tear you apart."

For mostly trusting me.

"I'm not killing him."

Even I didn't think that sounded very convincing. "Go," I said. "He'll be breathing when you get back."

Dash eased him down onto the floor and stood. "Don't fuck this up."

"I won't."

He jogged out of the room.

I kept my hand on Terric's chest, slowly, gently easing his heart into a more natural beat, then slower still, into sleep. If I let Death magic reach into him any deeper, he'd be hovering in a coma. More than that, he'd be comatose. After that: dead.

"You are not going to die on me, Conley," I said. "Not here and not now. You are going to heal. Do you understand that? Heal. All that Life magic in you that you use on everyone else has one job to do now. Heal you. This isn't goodbye. Got that?"

I sent Death magic gently into his body, his heart, bringing him very close to a coma state.

The remnants of pain between us finally eased. Here, in this state, he wasn't hurting. Hopefully, he could heal.

Here, in this state, my head cleared and Death magic backed off an inch.

"I will find the fuckers behind this," I promised him. "And I will tear them apart."

I didn't lift my hand from his chest, couldn't leave him half-dead and alone on this cold dirty floor. But I did shift so I could see the glyphs around the lawyer's corpse.

The answer to who was behind these killings, the answer to who was accessing such a brutal, twisted magic was right here. Drawn in dirt and flesh and death. The way to find that answer was here.

I didn't know why I hadn't realized it earlier.

We knew the deaths were linked. The actual glyphs on each of the dead were identical. So, too, the kind of magic that had killed them.

If the records Dash had dug up were correct, the people who had been killed were all connected, a part of the Pisces group.

All I had to do was follow those connections.

Through the glyphs that connected them. Through the magic that connected them.

I carefully gathered Death magic to my will, sent it plunging through the glyphs carved in the dirt, plunging through the glyphs carved in the dead body.

Connections and links worked both ways. Whether we liked it or not.

Magic poured out of me, burning down lines of old

magic like fire down gunpowder trails. It was dizzying, draining.

I felt like I'd just nicked an artery. But instead of losing blood, I was losing magic, draining down hard.

With that outpouring came knowledge. My vision swam with images of glyphs being drawn: drawn by wands that glowed with symbols carved into them. Flesh burned with the rancid, twisted magic, magic that leaped to the chants of voices, dozens of voices joined together.

And from that tangle of voices, of connections, of magic being dragged and twisted free from where we thought we'd safely locked it away, came one voice.

One face.

One magic user all the others were connected to.

One man behind the others.

"Fuck," I breathed.

The vision was hot-sharp.

I saw his face.

And he saw mine.

Connections work both ways. Whether we liked it or not.

Then the man I'd run into at Jak's place—Greg Padgett—lashed out with magic and broke the link.

CHAPTER 13

It wasn't easy, but it didn't take long to carry Terric up to the car. Dash had parked so close to the cabin door that all we had to do was ease Terric through it and into the back seat.

"Hospital?" Dash asked.

"Home. There isn't anything a doctor can do for him. Fucking magic. Give me a sec."

I strode back into the house, locked the basement door, then found a chain to loop through the front door handle I'd ruined. I focused Death magic on the chain links, heating them until they fused together, which was as good as it was going to get for locking the front door.

"I hate leaving all those damn magic books in there," I said as I ducked into the passenger seat. "Go."

"You think someone's going to take them? Use

them?" Dash started the engine and got the car turned so we could make the bridge.

"Fuck if I know. The magic that hit him? It's not magic I've felt before. Magic doesn't turn on like a light switch when you say a few bullshit words."

"That magic did. The old rules don't work anymore." He'd rolled across the bridge and was navigating the crappy dirt drive as quickly as possible.

Maybe the only way Greg, and whoever the hell else was in this with him, could dig magic free from the locks Terric and I had set on it was to twist magic, change it, use new ways to filter and pull on it.

Magic was a constant. It had always been in the world. Mankind had tried a lot of ways to reach it. The system of glyphs that the Authority and humankind in general had used to access magic had been deemed to be the easiest way to provide the desired results.

But it probably wasn't the only way. There were old stories of older cultures that had tried all sorts of things to access magic.

Spells, items, sacrifices.

Not all of them good.

"Is he...okay? Are you okay?" Dash asked as we hit the paved road at speed.

"He's healing. Not in pain right now. It tried to eat him. That magic."

"Fuck," Dash breathed. "You?"

"Fine. The spell didn't hit me."

"How bad are his wounds?"

I could lie. Tell him Terric would be fine. But I didn't know that. Didn't know what that magic had done to him. "I don't know."

Dash clenched his jaw and nodded once, his eyes never straying from the road.

"We'll find them," he said, low enough I almost didn't hear him over the engine's growl. "And we'll take them down."

I'll take them down, I thought. There was no way in hell I was going to put Dash at risk. But I could feel his heartbeat, the anger throbbing through him. He wanted someone dead for what they'd done to Terric.

I had every intention of making sure that happened.

———

"What the hell?" Jolie said. She rushed to hold the front door open for us. We carried Terric's unconscious body inside the house. "What the hell, what the hell?"

Her voice went up with each repetition.

"What. The. Hell?"

Dash, who was usually the calm and cool one in these kinds of situations, burned with anger and unbreakable silence.

"He's going to be okay," I said.

"Is he bleeding?" She pushed past us and opened the door on Terric's and Dash's bedroom. "Did you call 911? Should I call 911?" She fumbled for her phone in her pocket.

"No," I said, "and no." I nodded toward her phone. "And no."

Jolie moved across the room just ahead of us and pulled the covers down. We eased Terric down onto the bed.

Dash unlaced Terric's shoes, took them off.

"Someone better tell me what the hell happened, or I swear I'll call the cops."

Dash moved on to unbuckling Terric's belt, either unaware or completely ignoring that anyone else was in the room with him.

I took Jolie's arm and guided her out of the room and into the hall.

"No," she said. "I will not be shoved out of the way." She yanked her arm out of my grip and punched me in the shoulder. "Talk."

"Fuck, Jolie." I rubbed at my arm. She packed a punch.

She cocked her fist back and I left my hand defensively over my shoulder. She looked like the kind of woman who would hit in the exact same spot if given the chance.

"Talk," she repeated. "Why is my brother unconscious, half naked, and burned?"

"We went out to look into that lead on Harold Thorne."

"The lawyer? Did that damn lawyer do this?"

"No, that damn lawyer is dead."

"You killed him?"

"Found him. In the basement of the cabin. Long dead."

"From whom?"

"From what. Magic."

"No one can even access magic anymore," she said. "And you can't kill someone with magic."

She was angry, panicked, and gone so pale the red of her cheeks was the only color beneath her brittle blue eyes.

"Yes," I said, "I can."

She took a step back. There was more than fear on her face. "You *kill* people with magic? Is that why you came home with bullets in your chest? Is that why Terric is hurt? Fuck you, Shamus. I'm calling the cops."

I grabbed the phone out of her hand. Resisted the urge to drain down the energy in the battery. To kill it as easily as I knew I could.

I was trying to be reasonable here, trying not to lose control.

"No, you will not. The cops can't handle this. They

don't have the training. They don't have the magic. I can handle this. And I am going to—without getting anyone else involved."

She narrowed her eyes. I knew she wanted to argue, but I didn't have time.

"They told you Terric and I have a little bit of magic in us, right?"

She nodded.

"That magic in him is helping him heal. It's what it does. Stay here with Dash. Keep an eye on Terric. He needs time to heal and we're going to give him that." I handed her the phone.

Yeah, the battery was dead.

"Wait," she said, but I was already halfway across the living room.

"You can't go alone," she said. "Shame. Wait!"

But I was done waiting. I got into the car and left her, Dash, and Terric behind me.

CHAPTER 14

It wasn't hard to find Greg Padgett's place. A quick search on Google, a couple clicks, and I was parked outside his office.

He was a financial advisor of some sort. The sign bolted into the sandstone brick building said: Retirement Planning.

I sucked the heat out of a cigarette, then got out of the car, flicked the cig in the bushes and strode up to the front door.

Smelled like carpet glue or maybe new wallpaper inside. The young woman behind the counter at the back of the room glanced up as I walked in. She gave me a cool smile.

"May I help you?"

Guess I didn't look like a guy who was here to plan his retirement.

"I need to see Mr. Padgett."

Her smile didn't falter, but her eyes did a quick reassessment of me, my jeans, T-shirt, boots.

"I'm sorry," she said through her pleasant smile. "He's not available. Would you like to make an appointment?"

"No." I strode past her and through the door behind her. Ignored her warnings.

Short hallway. Three more doors. I knew exactly which door Greg was behind.

Strode to the end of the hall. Walked into his office, the woman right on my heels.

Greg sat behind a modern desk. He was scrolling through something on his screen. There were pictures on his walls. Pictures of Claire, pictures of their children, smiling, playing. Pictures of a happy family.

Fuck.

He glanced up, dark eyes taking me in and tightening with hate.

"You don't want her here," I said.

"I told him to leave," she said.

"It's all right, Tiffany." He stood. "Why don't you take the rest of the day off?"

"I...are you sure?" I could hear the frown in her voice but didn't turn to look at her. My eyes were on Greg alone. "I haven't finished the mailings."

"Mailings can wait for tomorrow," he said mildly. He wasn't looking at her either.

"All right," she said. "Thank you. I'll see you tomorrow." She strolled off.

I stuck my hands in the front pockets of my jeans. "You have fucked with the wrong man."

"I don't know what you mean."

"Found your friend, Harold, in his basement. Still don't understand why you people are leaving so damn much evidence around."

"What evidence? There is no crime."

"Tell that to the dead bodies you've littered across this city."

He shook his head. "It's not...you don't understand. What it's like not to...not to have what I need."

"Don't care what you need. But I will give you exactly what you deserve."

"Can you?" His voice dropped to a snarl. "Then do it! Break through the wall that's surrounding magic and get the hell out of my way."

"No. Not happening," I said. "There are too many people dead because of you. Too damn many people almost dead because of you."

I drew Death magic up out of the deep reservoir that filled me, let it whip and stretch into my bones, my blood. Let it fill my chest with a hungry heat. He would be so easy to end. To devour.

"I don't care how many people have died," he said. "I have to find a way to save my kid."

Death magic lashed inside me, wanting. But I heard him. Heard the anguish in his anger.

His kid? Claire's kid?

"Who?" I said.

"Lolly—Laura. Our youngest. She's ill." His mouth might have said *ill*, but his eyes said *dying*. "And there is nothing—*nothing*—I won't do to change that."

"Fuck," I said. "Fuck."

I could kill this guy. Make it look like a heart attack. It would be easy. Death magic turned in me, hungry for his life. Wanting his death. Wanting to kill Claire's husband, the father of their kids.

Hell.

I shoved the magic back into the core of me, breathed until I was sure it was going to stay there, until I was sure I had control.

"You have bought yourself one chance to explain to me *exactly* what you've done with magic. To whom. And for what," I said, breaking out into a cold sweat with the effort to hold magic at bay. "Talk as if your damn life depends on it."

Greg's lip curled up and I gave him a cold stare. I knew magic burned behind it, making promises I just might let it keep.

"Sit." I said, like he was nothing more than a dog. "Speak."

He hesitated, reconsidered. Sat.

I leaned my shoulder against the doorjamb and crossed my arms over my chest. Waited.

"It's...it's a rare disease," he said. "Of the blood. We didn't know she was sick until she was about three months old and couldn't gain any weight. Then we tried everything. Tests, doctors, specialists. Nothing."

He shook his head and swallowed as if the words were clogged there. "Nothing helps."

"So you started killing people with twisted magic," I said. "How in fuck is that helping your daughter?"

He shook his head, was still shaking his head. "The..." His voice dried up. He tried again. "I knew Harold most of my life. Knew he was involved in studying magic. How people used it, what it could do. It was a passion of his." His fingers were linked together, his eyes distant.

"When magic disappeared, it just made him dig deeper. Old texts, religions. I talked to him...about Lolly. If he could help us. If magic could help her. He convinced friends of his, fellow scholars who were all part of a...group that experimented with ancient magic rituals, to participate in an experiment."

So that explained the matching fish tattoos.

"Pisces," I said.

He nodded. "They agreed to complete a ritual he'd found. A linking of bodies, of life energy to draw on magic. To collect it and focus that life energy—to give that life energy to someone else."

I ground my teeth together. Idiots. Fucking idiots. Magic isn't some kind of cozy campfire to poke with a stick as you please. It's a bomb ready to take out as many people as possible at any given moment.

"How did that work out for them?"

"They're dead," he exhaled. "All of them. Harold thought if he used himself, his life, as the common thread connecting everyone together, that he would be able to regulate the spells. Regulate how much each of their lives poured out."

"Harold's dead."

He was back to nodding again. "He did that. Sacrificed himself to create the link. We didn't know. Didn't realize that's what he intended. When we found him, we didn't dare move him. Lolly was getting better. We thought if we touched him, changed anything, it all might fall apart. His death would mean nothing. She was so happy..."

"He's been dead for a year," I said.

He was gone, lost to memories. Maybe of his daughter's life, maybe of his friend's death.

"Hey." I snapped my fingers. "Why did the people in Pisces show up dead in the last few days? If this magic has been in place for over a year, why are they dropping like flies now?"

"I don't know." His eyes were dazed, all the fire in him gone to ash. "But I'll probably find out."

He drew open the collar of his shirt, revealing the tattoo of the fish over his heart.

———

He told me everything he knew. All the names of the people who were a part of Pisces and explained the ritual that had tied them together. Ink and Harold's blood had been used to draw a link through the fish tattoo—right over each of their hearts.

Vows, holy oils, and unholy herbs had done the rest to seal the link between the twelve of them.

The steady nature of the ritual did indeed mimic the concept of order and intent that glyphs used to draw in magic. It made a sort of sense that the ritual had worked.

I didn't doubt that Harold's death had sealed the deal and allowed for his life, and perhaps a portion of each of theirs, to support Lolly's.

"Why the wands?" I asked.

I was itching for a cigarette or a drink or something to kill. All three would be best. It seemed like I'd been standing in the cramped space of Greg's office beneath the suffocation of his guilt for hours.

"Wands?" He gave me a blank look. Shook his head. "We didn't have wands."

"Sure you did," I pressed. "You have wands and guns and chant."

He raised his eyebrows. "No wands. No guns. We did chant the vows back at the cabin, but that was the only time."

"Latin bullshit?"

"What?"

"The chanting?"

"English bullshit. A phrase repeated. Some kind of mantra for health, life giving to life."

"You didn't use wands?"

"No."

Hell.

"You've never used wands?"

"That's not how magic works, Shamus."

Double hell.

"I know," I said.

Two and two were not adding up here. Someone was using wands and magic together. The same words that had powered the wands had triggered that spell Terric drew.

There had to be a reason why the members of Pisces were dropping dead now.

It could be that the life span of the spell Harold cast had expired, and it was taking the hosts who were connected to it one-by-one.

Or it could be that there was another group out there looking for a way to break into magic for their own reasons and they'd happened on the same spells.

A group who had found a way to twist magic through those wands.

"Who is the head of Pisces?" I asked.

He shook his head. Looked miserable. "I don't know. I only joined—took vows of silence—after Harold told me he, and the group he was involved in might be able to help Lolly. I never asked those kinds of questions. Didn't really care."

"Can you ask them? Now?"

"Everyone I knew who was a part of it is dead."

He could be lying. But I could tell from his heartbeat and the remorse that shadowed his words that he wasn't.

"And your kid? Lolly?" I asked.

He shook his head. "She's...not well. Slipping. Already." He pinched his eyes with thumb and forefinger. "She's only two." He placed his head in his hands, fingers tugging at his hair. "What am I going to do? I can't go home. Not if...not if I'm next to die. I don't want them to see me that way."

Shit.

"Stay here. Let me handle it."

"What can you do?"

"We're about to find out." I turned, left his office.

He didn't call after me. Didn't do anything but sob.

This had just turned into something I didn't have a handle on. Something even I knew I was the wrong person to call upon to fix.

But there was no one else I could think of who could help.

For a moment, I wished things were the way they used to be. That everyone still had magic. In the old days, I'd hand this over to Zayvion to figure out. He was always cool-headed and smart when magic went to hell.

No matter how much I wanted to call on my best friend to bail me out, there was nothing he could do. He couldn't use magic.

Solving this was on me. All of it.

A little girl was dying. Someone out there had killed all the people who had tried to save her with both magic and their lives.

Her dad might be next in line.

I patted my pockets for my cigarettes. Nothing. Got in the car and slammed my fist into the wheel.

Fuck this. A little girl was dying. Claire's daughter.

If I knew what had triggered those spells the Pisces carried, if I knew how they'd been tapped and how they'd been killed, maybe I'd know how to keep the little girl safe.

I leaned my head back against the headrest. Scowled as I reached for the seatbelt then cussed when it scraped across my sore shoulder.

The shoulder I'd been shot in just a few days ago by that fucking sniper in the warehouse who had gotten away.

Something in my head finally clicked.

The sniper had left something behind. A broken wooden stick.

I reached over, checked the cup holder, then leaned down to feel across the floor. Finally found it where it had rolled onto the passenger side floor. Held it up to the light.

Not a stick. A wand.

Son of all the bitches.

I stared at it in my open palm. Licked my bottom lip.

If there was any magic in this, if any of the spell-work they had done to it was still intact, I could trigger it with my magic.

If I triggered it, would Greg go up in smoke? And if the last person tied to Lolly died, what would happen to her?

Maybe what was going to happen to her all along. He said she had been sick since she was born. Just because her dad had wild plans to find a cure for her wasn't a guarantee that she could actually be cured.

He didn't say the other Pisces deaths had injured his daughter. Not in an immediate sort of way. It seemed more like these people's lives, and the magic Harold Thorne had somehow created between them, was supporting her own body's will to survive.

If I tapped into the magic in the wand, I could use it to track the people who had admitted to killing the members of Pisces to find me. To find Terric.

All those Pisces people—people who were joined together in a common cause—a good, if misguided, cause—were dead because these wand wavers wanted to break through the walls of magic for their own purposes.

Over my dead damn body.

I rubbed at my forehead with my free hand. Took a breath and blew it out. This was going to take some finesse.

"Let's see where the hell you came from."

I was never very good at meditating. Couldn't empty my mind and body of thoughts and needs, couldn't come to peace with them either.

Still, I tried to think calm thoughts. Drew on the magic within me with fingertips. Light, careful. Sent just the faintest tendril of magic into the wand.

Spells stirred, that strange rotten orange stench I'd smelled before, filled the car.

The flash of a face, of the man who had held this wand, used it to channel twisted magic while he had a sniper's rifle trained on me, embedded itself into my mind.

Brown eyes turned down at the corners. Sandy hair, scar on the curve of his chin, square forehead. He had the look of a bored professor or someone who spent his waking hours cataloging stool samples.

I knew I could find him. And once I did, I could use him to find all the others.

Then I'd make it very, very clear to them that they were no longer allowed to use magic.

As for Lolly...well, a Death magic user wasn't going to be much help in healing her. Luckily, I knew the man who could.

I put the car in gear and headed for home.

CHAPTER 15

I knew there was something wrong two miles out. Something wrong with Terric. I stepped on the gas and ran a red.

Pain flared through our link and, along with it, a good deal of anger.

Terric was fighting someone, something.

Good news: he was conscious.

Bad news: he was in pain. That pain flashed bright, hot.

And then I didn't feel Terric at all.

I took the twisting road up the hill to my house on the edge, swung the car hard into the driveway.

The house door was open. It looked like it had been ripped off the hinges. Terric's car and Dash's truck were still in the driveway.

But I knew Terric was not in that house. I couldn't

feel his heartbeat. I couldn't feel the connection between us either. He was unconscious—had to be. I'd know if he were dead because I would feel it in my soul if he were no longer breathing in this world.

Someone was in there. Just one heart beating too slow.

I strode into the house. The smell of rotten orange hit me full in the face.

They'd done more than pull the door off the hinges, they'd tossed the place.

No one was in the living room or the hall.

The bedroom doors were flung open, broken bits of furniture scattered the floor.

I made straight for the kitchen.

They'd smashed a chair, tossed a couple more, shattered dishes. But I didn't care about any of that. There in the middle of the floor, in a small pool of blood, lay Jolie.

She was not moving, her heartbeat slow, her arm bent the wrong way below the elbow, a bruise spreading black and purple over her eye and split lip.

Anger slipped over that hot edge in my gut and exploded into rage.

Connections worked both ways. The wand brigade must have tracked the spell that hit Terric in the cabin back to here.

And there must have been a lot of them. Enough to

take out Terric and Dash. Enough to beat Jolie unconscious and leave her in her own blood.

I knelt and pressed my fingers to Jolie's throat. Her pulse was steady, her breathing even, if too slow. I checked her head. The cut, from where she'd hit something on the way down to the floor, was small but still bleeding.

I eased her broken arm against her chest then picked her up because I was all kinds of done with seeing Terric's little sister bleeding and broken on my kitchen floor.

She was supposed to be safe here. We were supposed to keep her safe.

She moaned softly, rolling her head against my shoulder. I hushed her, made soothing noises as I carried her down to my room and placed her gently on my unmade bed.

I pulled a cover over her, then went into the bathroom for a cloth and the prescription painkillers I had on hand. Found that, the elastic wrap bandage, and a sling in the medicine cabinet.

It took a little time and pressure to staunch the bleeding, then I bound her arm and got it in the sling.

"They took them," she said as I was adjusting the buckle on the sling.

"You're awake. Good." I handed her one of the pills

and the half empty beer on my nightstand. "Take it for the pain."

She washed the pill down with beer.

"I'm going to get you to the hospital."

"They took Terric," she repeated.

"Yeah." I took the beer from her, drained the rest of the bottle. "I'm going to go get him. First, you're going to the hospital."

"They had wands." Her voice was stronger. She pushed over and sat on the side of the bed. "What the hell, Shame? Wands only work in movies."

"Yeah, well, I guess wands work for assholes too. Think you can walk?"

"I think I can go with you to find Terric. And Dash."

"Nope."

Her mouth set and she very carefully stood. All the blood washed out of her face. I knew she was in a lot of pain. Still, she raised her chin. "Move."

"How are you going to be any use to Terric with a broken arm and a lump on your head?"

"Not even close to listening to you. If you won't drive, I will." She was halfway to the door and getting steadier with each step. The pain pills should be kicking in soon, but they weren't that fast.

"Do you think you can just drive down the street

and find them? They're dangerous, Jolie. Dangerous people don't make a habit of leaving trails."

"That's what I have you for. The way you and Terric are connected—whatever the hell that is—you know where he is, don't you?"

We were in the living room now. She was pulling Dash's coat off the hook by the busted door and sliding it over her shoulders one-handed.

"I don't take liabilities into fights with me. Especially when those liabilities are my friend's little sister."

"I know who they are." She walked out the door. "And I am nobody's liability, jackass."

Fuck.

"Tell me who they are while I drop you off at the ER."

"Nope."

I opened the passenger door for her and she slid into the seat without a complaint.

"You know I could knock you out and dump you anywhere I choose." I slammed the door as I got in behind the wheel. "This attack, this...wand and magic business doesn't concern you, Jolie."

"Yes, it does. Those weren't just any assholes waving wands. I've seen their faces before. At least three of them."

"Where?"

"Dealing for the Russian mob."

I turned the key and ground my way through the gears while I worked through that little snippet of information.

"You weren't telling us everything were you, Jolie?"

"I didn't think...didn't think it mattered what kind of shit the mob was involved in. Shit's shit, right?"

"Spill it. All of it."

"It wasn't just the drugs and human trafficking that freaked me out," she said. "I ran into some emails. Private emails. None of it made sense. Half of it was in Russian, but...well. I've taken Russian since high school."

"How fluent are you?"

"Enough to know that they weren't talking about a shipment of spices or drugs or people or weapons. They were talking about something else. About trying to tap into magic. About blowing things up until something shook loose."

"With wands?"

She nodded. "That wasn't in the emails, but yes. Those guys who blew the door off the hinges and kidnapped Terric and Dash might not be Russian, but they worked for the mob."

"What kind of mob hires out its dirty work?"

"All mobs," she said. "Easier to deal with transactions through middlemen. Why do you think they hired me? It wasn't for my personality." She hissed through her teeth at a particularly rough patch of road. "Do you have to hit every damn hole?"

"Hurt, does it? Notice that broken arm and knocked head? Good. Because those are the reasons you can get out now." I turned off the road and rolled up in front of the ER. "Get patched up, then call a cab and have it take you out to my mum's inn on the other side of the river. She'll take care of you."

"Screw that," she said. "If you drop me off here, I'll find you. I'm in this. All the way in this. I'm the reason those people with wands found you, and Terric, and Dash. I *caused* this, led them to all of you. No," she said as I tried to tell her otherwise.

She was angry, shaking.

"I left too many trails behind that they followed to you. My fault. And now Terric's in trouble. If we're going to the cops, I'll stand aside and let them handle it. But if we're going renegade vigilante, then I'm going to be there to fix this problem. My problem. I'm going to get my brother back. So you can drive or get out of my way."

She was dead set on this. That determined glint Terric usually got in his eye when he wasn't going to let me get away with shit flickered to life, hot with challenge.

"Jesus," I said, putting the car in gear and driving

away from the front of the ER. "You Conleys don't know when to quit, do you?"

"We quit when the job is done," she said. "So, let's get the job done. What's the plan?"

"I plan on walking into where ever they have taken him and killing anyone in my path to get to him."

She was silent. Maybe shocked.

Yeah, well, magic made for a cruel, cruel world and I had no problem being the cruel, cruel man who used it.

"How?" she asked.

"Things you don't want to know."

"Bet on that?"

"Things your brother doesn't want you to know."

"He's not here. How do you just walk in and kill people, Shame? Are you some kind of ninja?"

"Magic," I said simply.

She didn't say anything for a mile or so. I glanced over at her. The crease between her eyebrows wasn't from pain. The pills must be kicking in now and I knew they were good. She was still too pale, though. Still injured.

"Is that...part of what you and Terric have? Those dark looks you share when you think I'm not looking?"

She didn't know we were Soul Complements. It wasn't something that was talked about outside the Authority: two people who could use magic together in ways magic was never meant to be used. Two people who could break magic. Or in our case, lock it up so the rest of the world couldn't access it.

Well, shouldn't be able to access it.

"I can use magic," I said.

"Like him?"

I didn't say anything. She didn't need me to.

"Shit," she breathed. "Shit. They're going to figure that out, aren't they? They're going to do more than hurt him. They're going to...use him? Drain him?"

"Jolie," I said before she could think up nightmares that might very well come true. "I'm not going to let them do dick to him. Understand?"

She nodded, her eyes a little too wide.

"Another thing?" I added. "You're wrong. You weren't the cause of this. You weren't the reason they came looking for Terric and me. We are. We are the ones who shoved magic behind a wall no one can break. We're the ones who set the locks that keep it away from every other person in the world."

There it was. The secret we didn't want anyone to know. Not because we were afraid of people wanting to kill us for it—people always seemed to want to kill us for something. But because whoever knew what we had done, whoever carried that information, was in danger.

Just like Jolie was in danger.

"So what you're going to do is listen to me," I said. "I'm the expert here. On what magic can do. On what I can do with it. On what those asswipes think they can do with it. You are going to listen to me, follow my lead, and do what I say so I don't have to explain to Terric how his little sister got killed. Understand?"

"I can take care of myself."

"That's not what I'm saying and you know it. Listen to me. I want you alive at the end of this. Period."

"Okay." She nodded. "Okay. What do I do?"

"Let's find out where they have them locked up before we decide that. Have you received any contact from them?"

"No."

"Did they tell you why they took Terric and Dash?"

"It was...it happened so fast. They blew in, threw magic, and knocked out Dash. I was...I was hiding in the kitchen." She sounded miserable to admit it.

"You were smart not to throw yourself into the line of fire," I said. "Hands-on ass kicking is a little messier than cyber wars, and you were right to stay safe. After Dash was out, what happened?"

I took a turn toward the part of town where I could feel Terric. He was barely conscious. I had no idea about Dash.

"They found Terric. In the bedroom. He was still sleeping. He woke, though. When they started hitting him."

I eased down the street, eyes sharp for gunmen, wandmen too. My connection to Terric pulled me on.

"And?" I said.

"Jesus, Shame. They were beating on him."

I spared her a quick look. "He can handle it."

"Well, I couldn't. I couldn't see straight, I was so mad."

"Did you hit straight?"

"Damn right I did."

"Another thing I appreciate about a Conley."

I pulled the car into an alley and turned off the engine. "They're in that building over there."

"The hardware store?"

"Mexican restaurant being remodeled."

"How do you know?"

"I know."

"Okay. Now what?"

"Think you can handle a gun?"

She nodded. There was no panic, no fear in her eyes. "Won't be the first time."

"Good." I reached below the seat and pulled out the gun I knew Dash had stashed there. "You're going to walk behind me. Pay attention to any movement around us. Plug anyone I don't handle. Think you can do that?"

"Kill them?" Her voice was steady, but thin.

"I've found the shock of getting shot anywhere—arm, leg, stomach—is enough to stop most men cold. You don't have to kill them."

"I will...if I have to."

"You won't have to. That's not what you're here for." That was what I was here for.

We got out of the car. The wind was cool and heavy with the threat of rain, the light of the day already lowering into a dark, wet night. A drop of water hit my head, my hand.

I started across the street.

CHAPTER 16

"They'll see you," Jolie said as we crossed the street.

"I'm counting on it."

Death magic rolled out from me like the breath of winter hungry for the blood of spring. The world dissolved into hearts beating, life pumping out against the beat of time.

Seven men in the restaurant. Two women and a man in the hardware store. Forty-eight more people in the surrounding office buildings.

Didn't matter. None of them mattered. None of them would ever know that Death walked amongst them.

And that Death was in a very bad mood.

I knew Terric's heartbeat as well as my own. I felt Dash's too, scattered, fast. He was either afraid or furious. I'd bet cold cash on the latter.

"Stay close," I said. Jolie's heart beat hard with fear and adrenalin. She was right on my heels.

I kicked in the restaurant door. Strode into the darkened room. The rot of oranges hung heavy in the air. Death magic rolled out, searching, filling this space that was far too small for all this magic.

Five men waited in the shadows. They raised their guns.

Magic is fast. Bullets are faster.

But death cannot be stopped.

I clenched my fist around the wand in my coat pocket.

I couldn't kill with magic the way I used to—I had to have my hands on the person I intended to end—I had to have a connection to them.

No problem. I had the broken wand. The spells carved into it were connected to the same spells carved into the wands they carried.

Too bad for them.

If the wands could channel twisted magic, they could sure as hell channel Death magic.

Death magic arced like lighting through the wand I carried, searing into the wands in their hands. Death magic sank cold, greedy teeth deep into their hearts.

Fingers never closed on triggers.

Bullets never flew.

Four gunmen folded to the ground without so much as a scream.

Death magic drank them down as easy as water falling from the sky. I laughed with the sheer, glorious pleasure of it.

I wanted more. The anger in me, the death in me, wanted more. There was one man left. Paralyzed on the floor. He would be so easy to kill.

But I had other plans for him.

I could feel the drumming of Jolie's heartbeat—her fear, revulsion, and a thin thread of hope.

"Shame?" Her voice somehow pitched over the Death magic that roared through me. "Where's Terric?"

I must have been standing there for longer than I thought. The need for death, the sweetness of it, the satisfaction of it had distracted me.

I looked over my shoulder at her. Jolie's eyes were too wide, her face pale from shock and horror.

"Terric?" she said.

There were four dead men on the floor, but they weren't why we'd come here. Not really. She didn't need to see what I wanted to do to the fifth.

"That way." I pointed toward the kitchen.

"I'm not leaving you out here alone. You're coming with me," she said.

"Not yet." I closed in on the one guy who was still

breathing, heard Jolie's footsteps behind me. I knew it took everything she had to walk closer to the dead.

"Do you recognize him?" I asked as I stared down at the man.

He was in his mid-forties, dark skinned, and currently sweating from the agony of Death magic pinning him to the floor. He couldn't speak. He was damn lucky I was allowing him to breathe.

"Yes," Jolie said. "He was at the house."

I crouched down next to him. "You should be dead," I said. "I snap my fingers and you will be." I picked up his gun, removed the clip, then pulled the wand out of his frozen fingers, leaving my hand over his.

"Listen very carefully to me. You know who I am. I know who you are. I know who you work for. There is only one reason I'm going to allow you to live today. You are going to tell your bosses that the matter with Jolie Conley is over. You are going to tell them that if they so much as glance in her direction, if they so much as touch her or her brother, or anyone who I, Shamus Flynn, care about, I will walk through their front doors and I will kill them and everyone they love. As for these?" I pointed the wand at his face. Watched his eyes dilate. "These are mine."

I shot Death magic down the connections between every wand carved with the same symbols. All of the wands—maybe a dozen—were in Portland, which meant this hadn't had a chance to spread any farther yet.

Death magic devoured the wands, drained the magic, then sucked the vitality out of the wood.

The wand in my hand, and every other wand connected to it, turned to ash and dust. I crumbled it in my fist.

"Do we have an understanding?" I pulled my hand away, simultaneously reining in Death magic, giving him the ability to move, to talk, but not taking the pain away.

"Yes," he blurted out. "I understand."

"Good." I stood. "If you ever touch my people again, I will tear you apart into pieces and make sure you live long enough to feel every second of your long, agonizing death. Now get the hell out of here."

He rolled onto his side, got up on his feet and staggered out the door.

I would know where he went. I would know who he went to. He was marked by Death magic, an easy target. He was a dead man walking.

I still didn't like letting him go.

"Shame?" Jolie said.

"This way." I strode through the room to the kitchen in the back.

Dash was gagged and handcuffed to a chair. He

made a sound when I came in, eyes filled with warning.

Someone had used him for a punching bag and that pissed me the hell off.

"They're dead," I said. "Hold on." I heard Jolie move in behind me, then off to the right where I knew she'd find Terric unconscious.

I heard him groan. Okay, not quite unconscious.

"Shame," she called. "You need to look at this."

"Hold on." I flipped out my keychain with a hand-cuff key on it. Used it to unlock Dash from the chair. "You okay, Dash?"

"Fine. Where's Terric?"

"He's breathing. Back there. Stay put. I'll be right back."

I strode to the far side of the kitchen where Jolie leaned against the open pantry door. She hadn't stepped into the room yet.

"Let me see." I moved past her. Stopped.

Dash had not stayed put. He was right behind me and swore when he looked in the room.

Terric lay in the middle of the floor, stripped down to his waist. Carved into the floor around him were the symbols I'd last seen around the dead lawyer in the basement of the cabin. Burned across his chest was the glyph for Proxy and Surrender, and across his fore-head: Binding.

"Son of a damn bitch," I snarled. "Son of a bitch."

They had set Terric out just like Harold Throne. They had intended to sacrifice, to use him as the key to slip the lock and break magic free. And if not that, they would have just funneled all the magic out of him they could before he died.

Since he carried Life magic in his body, it would have been years of pain before Terric gave up and became nothing more than a shriveled corpse.

"I am getting sick of finding you half dead, Ter." I walked over the glyphs surrounding him, wished I could erase them forever, burn them out of the concrete they were burned into.

Terric moaned again and his eyes rolled, too much white at first, then sliding down into a sightless blue.

"I got you," I said as magic in him pushed against the glyphs that bound him.

I knelt at his side. With control I wasn't sure I had, I traced each of the glyphs on his skin backward, canceling them with Death magic. It wouldn't erase them from his flesh, but it would break the binding.

I slashed a finger across the length of each: chest, neck, and forehead.

Terric took a huge gasping breath. Magic flared in him so hot and fast he glowed with a burning blue light.

Life magic.

"Easy," I said. "You're fine. We got you."

"Jolie?"

"You know she's here. Right here."

That was all it took for her to rush into the room, kneel by his side, and help him sit.

I couldn't tell which of them was more worried about the other. But I knew which of them calmly hushed his sister and with shaking hands healed her broken arm, mended her cut head, and soothed her with gentle words.

She helped him up onto his feet.

That's when he got a look at Dash standing right behind her.

"Dash," he said quietly.

Dash smiled. His swollen lip split open and sent a bright flash of blood down his chin. "Good to see you, babe."

He took the few steps to Dash, Jolie right beside him, her arm still around his waist, his over her shoulder. He reached out for Dash. "I'm sorry—"

Dash shook his head. From how pale he suddenly went, that probably hadn't been such a good move. "Wouldn't be anywhere else. Wouldn't be with anyone else. No matter the cost."

Terric placed his fingertips gently on the side of Dash's face.

Dash didn't wince at that contact.

"I love you," Terric whispered.

Dash just swallowed and nodded.

Jolie slid out from under her brother's arm and Terric wrapped it instead around Dash, pulling him close. Then Terric bent to him, shifted his mouth so he could carefully, gently kiss him.

Dash made a soft sound. It was not made out of pain.

I'd always wondered what it would be like to be touched that way, kissed intimately by someone who was Life magic, who was living, healing, tenderness.

Looked like it was not a bad thing at all.

I would have walked out of the room and given them some privacy, but they were blocking the damn doorway.

Jolie stepped over to me and handed me my gun. "I don't know what you did even though I saw it with my own eyes," she said. "I don't know how you did it, but thank you, Shame."

And then she draped her arms over my shoulders and planted a very hot, very thorough, and very sexy kiss on my mouth.

The sound I made as I kissed her back wasn't from pain either.

CHAPTER 17

I walked into the pediatric waiting room at the hospital on a sunny, bright morning. I had two cups of coffee in my hand. A man and woman sat leaning against each other in the small waiting area. From the pile of empty cups and coats folded into makeshift pillows, it looked as if they had spent the night in the chairs.

"Greg?" I said, with cheerful, if fake, surprise. "I thought I'd find you down here. How's Lolly doing?"

He blinked blurry eyes red from lack of sleep—maybe from tears too—and frowned at me.

"Promised I'd check in on you, remember?" I said, offering him one of the coffees. "Back at your office the other day?"

"Uh..." he said as he took the coffee and glanced over at his wife, Claire. "Right. I remember."

"Shame?" Claire's voice broke. "What are you

doing here? I didn't even know you were in town. It's been..."

"...a long time," I finished for her. "It's good to see you, Claire."

She smiled a little and tucked her mussy hair back behind her ears. She sat forward and straightened her T-shirt over a belly just beginning to round with life.

"I work in the neighborhood with your husband," I said. "Heard about your little girl and thought I'd come by and offer up some early morning courage. Coffee, cream, and extra sugar."

Just how she liked it.

"Oh." She took the cup I offered. "Thank you. That's really nice of you. I didn't know you knew Shame," she said to Greg.

"We just ran into each other," I said. "Say, Greg, do you feel like stretching your legs?"

He stood, the coffee in his hand forgotten. "Sure." He sounded like he was ready to face down death—whether his daughter's, or his own. "I'll be right back, honey."

"Really good to see you, Claire," I said, trying to keep it light.

I didn't wait to see if the confusion and guilt cleared from her eyes.

I led the way at an easy stroll down the hall, past the larger waiting room, and off into a side corridor which ended with a fantastic view of the hills over Portland.

"Here's how this is going to go," I said as we both stared out the window. "I'm going to remove those glyphs you let them cast on you—and yes, I can do that—and you are going to stay away from the Pisces and magic. All magic."

"Why would I do that?" he asked. "I'm all she has left."

I gave him an even stare. "If you keep your hands off magic, if you keep your mouth very, very shut, I will see that your daughter is healed. And no, I'm not going to tell you how."

I felt Terric enter Pediatric Intensive Care. Felt the Life magic flowing from his hands, healing. Healing a little two-year-old girl.

"If you ever speak of it to anyone, even your wife, I will take this gift away."

I tipped my head down and let Death magic press cold knuckles into his spine. "Do you understand me?"

He nodded, and a tear tracked out of the corner of his eye, maybe from exhaustion, maybe from relief.

"Save her," he begged. "If you can save her, I'll do anything. Anything you ask."

"Good. Let's find a private room. You're gonna strip so I can cancel those spells."

———

Miraculous recovery. Total remission. The doctors couldn't explain it. The doctors didn't have to.

Greg kept his mouth shut, took his happy wife and healthy daughter home. Last I heard, he was looking into how to get the fish tattoo removed too.

"That is a lot of boxes," Jolie announced as she clomped up the stairs from the basement.

"Not my fault the lawyer hoarded things much too dangerous to keep in a cabin." I sat on the couch, drinking a beer and watching some movie where a giant monster destroyed a vacation paradise.

"You're just lucky I'm sticking around to catalogue it all," she said.

"You are not staying. You are going back up to Seattle to school."

"Nope. Transferred. I'm a Portlandian now."

I groaned. "There is no more room in this house. I want my life back. I want my living room back."

"Poor selfish baby," she cooed.

"Poor?"

"What, you have a real job?"

I grinned. "I get by."

"It just so happens I found a place downtown. Not too far from here. Walking distance to everything interesting. Low rent and nice enough. I'll invite you over once I settle in. I expect a hell of a housewarming gift."

"You'll get a second-hand re-gift, if you're lucky."

"After everything I did for you?" She crossed the room and dropped down onto the couch like she owned it, propping her sneakers up next to mine on the coffee table which was scattered with a few paperback novels, her tablet, and a couple of things I thought she might use to hold back her hair.

She looked good there. Comfortable. At home. And while this damn house was in no way big enough to take in another Conley, I realized I liked having her around.

I'd never admit it to her, but I was glad she would be staying in town.

"All you did for me was get me mixed up with the Russian mob and their wand-wielding henchmen. Who, by the way, shot the crap out of me and ruined my favorite T-shirt."

She shrugged one shoulder and tried not to look guilty about that. "All your T-shirts are exactly the same. And you would have gotten shot anyway, right?"

"Maybe not by the Russian mob if some smartass hacker hadn't screwed with their bank accounts."

"About that. The whole mess..."

"The part where you stole funds from the mob, or

the part where you didn't tell us you knew magic was involved?"

"All of it. I was in pretty deep. I don't know how I would have gotten out without you and Terric and Dash."

We'd gotten news back from the Russians. They had agreed to cut their losses and leave Jolie, and everyone connected to her, alone for a lifetime or two.

"You would have managed," I said, "but I'm not sure if the outcome would have been as favorable. Or as easy."

"That wasn't anywhere near easy. Terric almost died. So did you."

I made a rude sound. "Yeah, well, neither of us are any good at staying dead for long."

"I mean it, Shame. I didn't have any right to drop this on your doorstep, but I did. And I want to thank you. Thank you for helping me. Thank you for saving my life."

She looked like she was on the edge of tears.

It had been a couple days since we'd had to go kill anyone, and all of us were healed—physically anyway—including all those glyph marks on Terric. But these kinds of experiences, when the whole world turns upside down and gets bloody and horrible, can change a person.

I knew her world would never be the same again.

"You're welcome," I said simply, even though in some ways I thought maybe I ought to be the one who apologized to her.

"That's it?" she asked.

I raised an eyebrow. "There should be more?"

"Seems like you might...want something?" She tipped her head up, gave me an even stare.

I didn't know what she thought she was offering, with that look in her eyes. "I want you to move out so I can have my damn couch back. One Conley in this house is one too many."

"Well, maybe I want to give you something." She stood, her gaze holding mine.

I took another drink of my beer. Waited.

"Something I've been thinking about the last couple days." She stepped over my legs, so she was straddling them. Bent so that her hair swung forward across her cheeks and her T-shirt opened at the collar to slip me a peek at the black lace of her bra.

"Oh?" I managed, though my mouth had gone dry.

"I only got one try, but I liked the taste of you." She whispered it and my heart went too hot, my pulse too fast.

She leaned in a little closer, so that her perfume and the candy scent of her lip balm filled my senses.

I opened my mouth, waiting for her lips, wanting her mouth on mine so I could taste her back.

"Hey," Dash called out as he walked through the front door. "Got the last load of boxes out front. Could use a hand unloading."

He paused once he caught sight of Jolie and me.

"Unless you're busy or something?"

Ass.

Jolie bit her bottom lip and smiled. "Too bad," she murmured. "That might have been fun."

I lifted a hand, but she was already straightening, stepping over my legs and walking toward Dash. "I'm not busy or something," she said. "I'll help."

She strolled across the room and out into the sunshine.

Damn. It.

Dash gave me a look. "Really, Shame?"

"Hey, she started it. I was sitting here. Innocently."

"Innocently?"

"Innocently."

"Who's innocent?" Terric asked, walking into the room.

Terric was healed now and looked like he'd never had a mark on him in his life. Dash too. As a matter of fact, I had heard just how thorough Terric had been about going over every inch of Dash's body the last couple nights.

I needed to soundproof my room.

"Shame is innocent, apparently," Dash said.

Terric slipped his arm around Dash and Dash returned the favor, leaning into him a bit. They looked good together. Relaxed. Happy. I wondered if they were done fighting about Dash moving out.

"So, when are you two moving out?" I asked.

"We're not," Dash said. "I talked to the company. They're fine with me working freelance from home. I'm thinking about converting a corner of the basement into an office."

I groaned and pushed up out of the chair. "Were you going to run that by me? Maybe I have plans for the basement. Plans for *my* basement."

Terric shrugged. "Consider it run by you." He released Dash, who grinned and walked out the front door to help with the unloading.

"Hell," I said without any heat. "So. You two figured it out? The job thing?"

Terric nodded. "I was being an idiot about it. Luckily, I got over it. Plus, the way things are now, there was no way he was going to leave."

"The way what things are now?"

"The Russians can't be the only ones looking to break into magic. Even if we lock all the books in the basement, people will keep trying to reach magic. People have always tried to find magic, have always wanted to use it."

I nodded. "That's not all that different than a month ago."

"But now we know they've found a way. Those wands…"

"You and I will know if anyone uses anything connected to them. Connections work both ways."

He crossed his arms over his chest. "Which means you and I are now the guardians of magic. You know that, don't you? We're the guardians of that secret lore we're U-Hauling into the basement. Guardians of innocent people—children—not being hurt and killed by those who break and twist magic just to have magic."

"We broke magic," I reminded him.

"We broke magic to save magic. To save people."

"So, you're suggesting that we, what? Start a new secret group? Revive the secret Authority again?"

"Something like that." His gaze was even, blue, bright with intelligence and caring and Life magic.

"And who, exactly, are you going to allow into our new secret magic club?"

"Just you and me."

"And Dash?"

"And Dash," he agreed.

"What about your sister?"

"She doesn't need to be mixed up in something as dangerous as the guarding of magic."

"She's already mixed up in it. I think she can handle it."

"Vote of confidence?" he said. "Out of you? Is she blackmailing you?"

"N-no." I stuttered.

His eyes narrowed dangerously. "Is there something going on between you?"

"C'mon, Terric," I said, side-stepping that question like a boss. "You know I can't be blackmailed. I don't care about anything enough for someone to threaten me with it. But she's smart, she's been through a hell of a lot with us over the last couple days. And she's going to catalogue all those magic books for us. How do you suggest we keep her *out* of our secret group?"

"Shit," he said. "Shit."

"Don't worry, big brother. Our secrets are safe with her."

Jolie strode into the room, a box of books in her arms. "Are you two still standing here?"

Dash strolled in behind her, pushing a dolly stacked with boxes. "It'd go a lot faster if the two of you helped unload," he said.

"Someone has to supervise," Terric and I said at exactly the same time.

Jolie snorted. "Weird."

Dash shook his head. "Fine. Supervise lunch, would you? I'm starving."

They crossed to the hall, then I heard them take the stairs down.

"You do it," I said, walking back to the couch and snagging up my beer.

"It's your turn to cook," Terric said.

"Rock, paper, scissors?"

"You are such a child." But he placed his fist in his palm.

Terric threw paper, I threw scissors.

"Ha!" I said.

He sighed. "You know I threw that game. You're a terrible cook, Shame, and none of us should eat the result of your failure."

"Well, then why don't you whip me up a steak, rare, with a nice pile of fresh cut fries on the side, Lord Chef."

"You're getting gravel and dirt. Maybe. I might let you pour ketchup on it if you stay out of my way while I work."

"Make it quick, your Highness."

"Blow me, Shame."

"What? So soon? I thought you and Dash last night..."

He walked toward the kitchen and bent his hand behind his back to flip me the bird.

I grinned, took a swallow of beer.

Something crashed in the basement, followed by

laughter. Terric paused for a second, maybe checking to see if there were any broken bones that needed healing. Then he stepped into the kitchen humming, content and unconcerned.

I propped my foot up on the coffee table and turned up the volume on the movie.

Some people don't die easy.

I knew I was surrounded by those kinds of people. Strong people.

Survivors. Companions. Family.

And that, sure as hell, was worth living hard for.

———

Want to read more from Devon?

Sign up for her fun newsletter and find her newest books at: www.DevonMonk.com

ACKNOWLEDGMENTS

This book has a special place in my heart. Shame and Terric go through a *lot* in books 1 & 2 of this series, and here, they finally get a chance to explore life and magic in a new way. I had so much fun revisiting these two trouble makers. I hope you enjoy seeing them again too!

Big thank you to my first readers, Dejsha Knight and Dean Woods, for your insight and patience. You are both amazing.

Huge shout-out to Sharon Elaine Thompson for her excellent copy editing, and to my sharp-eyed proof-reader Eileen Hicks.

To the incomparable artist Lou Harper at Cover Affairs: thank you for lending your talent to this series.

I am forever grateful to all my family who told me not only "yes" but also "it's about time" when I wondered if I should continue on with Shame and Terric's story.

To my husband, Russ, and youngsters Kameron and Mike, Konner and Anna (and little Phoebe) you are the best part of my life. I love you.

And to you, dear reader. Thank you for sharing this exciting journey with me.

ABOUT THE AUTHOR

Devon Monk is a USA Today bestselling fantasy author. Her series include Ordinary Magic, Souls of the Road, West Hell Magic, House Immortal, Allie Beckstrom, Broken Magic, and the Age of Steam steampunk series. Her short fiction can be found in various anthologies and in her collection: A Cup of Normal.

Devon lives in lovely, rainy Oregon. When not writing, she is drinking too much coffee, watching hockey, or knitting ridiculous things.

ALSO BY DEVON MONK

SOULS OF THE ROAD

Wayward Souls

Wayward Moon

Wayward Sky

WAYWARD STORIES

Oak and Ink

ORDINARY MAGIC

Death and Relaxation

Devils and Details

Gods and Ends

Rock Paper Scissors

Dime a Demon

Hell's Spells

Sealed with a Tryst

At Death's Door

Nobody's Ghoul

Brute of All Evil

WEST HELL MAGIC

Hazard

Spark

Graves

BROKEN MAGIC

Hell Bent

Stone Cold

Backlash

Dirty Work

HOUSE IMMORTAL

House Immortal

Infinity Bell

Crucible Zero

AGE OF STEAM

Dead Iron

Tin Swift

Cold Copper

Hang Fire (short story)

ALLIE BECKSTROM

Magic to the Bone

Magic in the Blood

Magic in the Shadows

Magic on the Storm

Magic at the Gate

Magic on the Hunt

Magic on the Line

Magic without Mercy

Magic for a Price

SHORT STORIES

A Cup of Normal (collection)